Blinking in confusion, Julia couldn't make sense of his words.

"Act like you know me and I'll handle the rest," he continued, his eyes locking on hers.

When Julie had been six years old she'd left the back door of their Mississippi home open and a rattler had slithered inside. When she'd seen the snake in the kitchen a few minutes later, she'd screamed so loudly the yard man had run into the house without even knocking. He'd compensated for his lapse in protocol by dispatching the unwanted guest.

Since her marriage, she'd often thought she'd let another snake into her life.

Now Julia had the feeling she'd done it once again.

Dear Reader,

Our children are our most precious possessions, even though one might argue they are not possessions. We argue over them, though, as if they were, making them pawns in our battles, whether we mean to or not. The reason for their importance in these awful situations is obvious. We love them so much we are willing to lie, steal, cheat and possibly even kill for them.

Not Without Her Son is the story of a woman who is willing, able and prepared to do all of the above and more. Julia Vandamme, the victim of a ruthless man and her own bad choices, finds herself imprisoned in a foreign country with her son, Tomas. She's married, she's trapped and she's desperate. The last thing she wants is her son to become his father. For Julia Vandamme *nothing* comes before her son, including her own life.

Wouldn't it be great if every parent felt this way? What would it mean to the world if everyone who was a parent put their children first? *What if nothing mattered but our kids?*

I was lucky enough to have a mother and father who gave their all to me, my sister and my brother. Believe me, they gave so much of their love and attention that there were plenty of times all three of us wished for parents who would just leave us alone! And when they couldn't be there, their own parents took over.

Families are the building blocks of our society, and if you put your child above everything else, like my parents and the heroine in this book, then you're performing the most important job in the world. I hope you enjoy this story and find inspiration in it, as well.

Kay David

NOT WITHOUT HER SON
Kay David

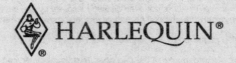

HARLEQUIN®

TORONTO • NEW YORK • LONDON
AMSTERDAM • PARIS • SYDNEY • HAMBURG
STOCKHOLM • ATHENS • TOKYO • MILAN • MADRID
PRAGUE • WARSAW • BUDAPEST • AUCKLAND

ISBN 0-373-71303-7

NOT WITHOUT HER SON

This edition published by arrangement with Harlequin Books S.A.

® and TM are trademarks of the publisher. Trademarks indicated with
® are registered in the United States Patent and Trademark Office, the
Canadian Trade Marks Office and in other countries.

www.eHarlequin.com

Printed in U.S.A.

Books by Kay David

HARLEQUIN SUPERROMANCE

798–THE ENDS OF THE EARTH
823–ARE YOU MY MOMMY?
848–THE MAN FROM HIGH MOUNTAIN
888–TWO SISTERS
945–OBSESSION
960–THE NEGOTIATOR*
972–THE COMMANDER*
985–THE LISTENER*
1045–MARRIAGE TO A STRANGER
1074–DISAPPEAR
1131–THE TARGET*
1149–THE SEARCHERS
1200–SILENT WITNESS
1230–THE PARTNER

UPCOMING TITLES IN THE OPERATIVES SERIES

NOT WITHOUT THE TRUTH
NOT WITHOUT CAUSE

SIGNATURE SELECT SAGA

NOT WITHOUT PROOF

*The Guardians

This book is dedicated to the memory of my mother and father, Pauline and Earl Cameron. Their legacy was priceless and their love will never fade.

CHAPTER ONE

San Isidro, Colombia

JULIA VANDAMME-RAMIREZ LOOKED over the crowd milling about her living room. Sipping drinks and eating hors d'oeuvres, her guests, all dressed expensively if not tastefully, mingled and laughed, clearly enjoying themselves. She smiled tightly and waved to one of the women, catching her husband's attention with the motion. Miguel followed Julia's gesture, then he turned in her direction and gave her a slight nod.

Julia acknowledged him and drew a deep breath, relief washing over her at his approval. Standing by Julia's side, Meredith Santera looked out over the crowd in obvious amazement. She was Julia's best friend. Julia's only friend...from before.

"Where on earth did these people come from?" Meredith asked. "Surely they don't all live in San Isidro?"

"They live all over," Julia answered. "They come to San Isidro because San Isidro is where we live. If they want to do business with Miguel—and they all do—then they make the trip."

"They're business associates?" Meredith sounded doubtful. "Including the old broad over there who's laughing so loud?"

"Not her. She's the governor's wife." Her mask of gaiety intact, Julia waved at someone else then spoke under her breath. "But Miguel told me to be especially nice to her. I guess he wants something from them." She smiled and dipped her head at someone else. "But if I don't get out of here in the next two minutes, my head is going to explode."

Meredith mimicked Julia's nod to Miguel and spoke graciously, her slow drawl reflecting the Southern past they shared. "Then shall we retreat to the patio? If you're gonna do something messy, we might be better off outside."

Julia grinned, her expression authentic this time. "Good point." She tilted her head to the French doors at their back. "Let me grab another glass of wine and I'll meet you on the patio. We have a lot of catching up to do. It's been way too long."

Meredith murmured her consent before sliding away soundlessly. Handing her empty flute to a passing waiter, Julia waded into the crowd and continued to greet as many people as she could, her mood lifting as she anticipated visiting with her friend. The last time they'd seen each other had been at Julia's wedding, almost four years ago. She still couldn't believe her good luck—if she hadn't left that department store in Bogota at just the right time, their paths would have never crossed. As it was, Julia had cried her friend's name and grabbed her in a tight hug, impulsively insisting she come to their party a few nights later. Miguel had not been happy about it, but he'd finally relented, realizing it would have created more of a problem to uninvite her.

Reaching the bar, Julia accepted a new glass of merlot, then headed for the rear of the room. She was almost to the doors when Miguel's fingers slipped around her elbow and he pulled her to a stop.

"You aren't going to the terrace, are you, darling? We have other guests in addition to your friend, you know."

His voice was low and husky, as full of charm as ever. Julia's heart skipped a beat because she knew what was coming.

"I don't think those other guests would appreciate it if I threw up on them." She met his black eyes and wondered how she'd ever thought them sexy. "I'm getting a migraine. I need some fresh air."

"I'm sorry," he said politely. He always spoke this way to her. Anyone who listened would be impressed by his smooth civility. She had been when they'd met. "I hope it doesn't intrude on your time tomorrow with Tomasito."

But she heard the threat, just as he knew she would. Miguel controlled everything in her life, including the amount of time she spent with their three-year-old son, Tomas. When Julia didn't behave as Miguel thought she should, he punished her by cutting her visits short or eliminating them all together.

Her mouth went dry. "Tomas expects me, Miguel. I told him we were going to have a picnic."

"Then you'd better not break your promise." To make his point even clearer, he tightened his grip on her arm. Refusing to change her expression, Julia endured his painful touch.

"Please visit with my guests. *All* of them."

He left her standing alone and shaken. With no other option, she sent a quick look through the windows. Meredith had seen the encounter and clearly understood. She mouthed the words *Go on,* then pointed to a side door and held both hands up, her fingers splayed.

Meredith and Julia had met between Julia's junior and senior year in high school when Meredith's family had been transferred to Pascagoula, her father a Naval officer, her mother an Argentinian expat. Julia was the younger of the two by four years, but she'd been home schooled and was much more mature than most kids her age. She'd been thrilled to meet the exotic, world-traveling Meredith, and they'd hit it off immediately. As fall had approached, Meredith had convinced Julia to apply to the same college at which she would be enrolled as a junior—the University of Southern Mississippi. They'd developed the finger flash, a code for skipping out, in a boring history class they'd shared. All ten fingers meant "ten minutes."

Julia nodded then held her own hand up, adding five more. Miguel would expect her to do exactly as he'd instructed and he'd check to make sure she complied, but if she put on a show for at least fifteen minutes, she'd be all right. He would be involved in something else by then.

Sure enough, by the time she'd made a second circuit of the room, Miguel had disappeared. She glanced up the staircase to his office. The lights were on and the doors were closed. He was obviously holding one of his endless meetings. If she still thought he was the Colombian diplomat he'd claimed to be, she wouldn't have given his absence another thought, but she noticed it now, because she knew the truth.

Picking up the hem of her beaded dress, Julia hurried through the kitchen and walked outside. She had just crossed the center of the patio when a shadow materialized from beside the house.

Julia stumbled back in fright and gasped, putting a hand to her chest before she recognized her friend. "Good God, you scared me half to death, Meredith. When did you learn to be so quiet?"

Meredith shrugged and waved off Julia's comment. "Miguel didn't look too happy. I didn't want him to see me." She tilted her head to the window above. "He's in his office, isn't he?"

"You've become observant, too." Julia looked up, as well. "He's having some kind of meeting. He does that a lot when we entertain. I hardly see him anymore, even when he's here, which isn't often."

"That's unfortunate." Meredith's voice was neutral in the darkness. "You must get lonely."

Julia knit her fingers together. There was no one she was closer to than Meredith, but Julia's relationship with her husband had never been a topic of discussion between them. For one thing, Meredith didn't like Miguel and Julia knew it. For another, she'd been raised not to air her dirty laundry. Vandammes didn't talk outside the family, especially about trouble.

Even as she had these thoughts, however, Julia acknowledged, at least to herself, the real reason she'd stayed silent—she was embarrassed. How could she have made such a horrific mistake? How could she have missed the monster beneath the facade?

"It's a quiet life," Julia finally replied. "But I have Tomas."

"What about friends?" Meredith asked. "We haven't talked for a long time. Have you gotten close to any of the women inside?"

"They're very busy," Julia said. "Everyone has so much to do with the children and everything."

"The children?" Meredith didn't bother to hide her skepticism, her voice turning sharp. "They've all got nannies, Julia. Nannies and cooks and maids and God knows what else, just like you do. How busy can they be?"

On edge already, Julia felt her throat go tight. She turned away from her friend. She couldn't explain. Not now.

"Oh, shit. Julia, honey, I'm sorry. I didn't mean anything by that—"

She reached out to turn Julia around, her fingers pulling at Julia's right elbow. Julia winced as a streak of pain raced up her arm.

"My, God, what's wrong? Did I hurt you?"

"It—it's nothing," Julia lied. "I—I fell against the door the other day and my arm's still bruised, that's all."

Meredith froze and without saying a word, pulled back Julia's sleeve. Even in the faint light that fell from Miguel's office, the fingerprints were obvious. Meredith let the fabric drop, then she raised her suddenly hard gaze to Julia's. "What in the hell's going on here? A door doesn't leave a bruise like that."

"It's nothing," she insisted.

"Nothing, my ass." Meredith shook her head in disgust, then jerked her thumb toward the window above them. "He did that to you, didn't he?"

Julia debated how to answer, a heavy silence building between the two women. After a moment, she spoke. "You can't do anything about this, Meredith. It would be best if you forgot what you just saw."

"Best for who?" she snorted. "Not you, I'm sure."

During their college years, everyone had called Meredith a superwoman because she'd righted every wrong she came across, regardless of the consequences. The last thing Julia needed was Meredith getting involved in her problems. The very last thing.

"I'm not important here, Meredith. Okay? And nothing is going to change that. Not even you."

"If you're not important, who is? The wife beater up there?"

"My son is," Julia said, her voice vehement. "And I have to remember that above everything else."

"Take him and leave."

"It's a little more complicated."

"Nothing's *that* complicated," Meredith retorted. "Unless he keeps you a prisoner or something."

With three glasses of wine and nerves stretched wire-thin, Julia felt her defenses slip, Meredith's opening too perfect to resist. "Not 'or something,'" she said grimly. "A prisoner is exactly what I am. He has my passport, all the cash, everything. I can't leave."

Meredith showed so little reaction it made Julia wonder why, but there was no stopping her now, her reckless words rushing out in a torrent. "It's been that way from the beginning. I hate Miguel Ramirez with every bone in my body. If I could, I'd kill him with my bare hands and never look back."

MEREDITH STARED at Julia with a gaze steady enough to be unnerving. Between the sudden tenseness and the dim light, she almost seemed a stranger. "Tell me more," she commanded.

"There's nothing more to tell," Julia answered, her anger changing into bitterness. "Miguel is a very controlling, very angry man and I do what he says because I have no choice."

"C'mon, Julia Anne. Everyone has a choice—"

Julia held up her hand. Meredith was the only person who ever used her middle name, and hearing it now brought back their dormitory days and the whispered confidences they'd shared in the middle of the night. Back then, their biggest problem had been how to arrange the loss of Julia's virginity. As she thought of the hell her life had become, a bubble of hysteria formed in her throat, but she pushed it down.

"Tomas is the only thing I care about, and I would never leave him."

"Take him with you."

"I can't. I have no funds, no assets, nothing. Even if I did manage—"

"Do your parents know what's going on? I can't believe they wouldn't help you."

Julia's jaw tightened. She'd been out of college for a month when she'd met Miguel at a Fourth of July party at a hotel in Atlanta. Her father had argued stridently against the relationship and her mother's disapproval had been just as vehement, if less vocal. But tired of watching her friends pair off one by one, and lonely as well, Julia had ignored what she thought of as her father's overprotectiveness and her mother's snobbery. She'd married Miguel within weeks of their introduction.

Julia had come to think the impulsive act—so out of character for her—had been an unconscious effort to spite her parents and their restrictive nature. If it had been, the trick had backfired. She'd hurt no one but herself.

She shook her head. "I haven't heard from Mother and Daddy in months and frankly, even if I did, it wouldn't make any difference. All the money in the world wouldn't keep us safe. Miguel would find us and when he did…"

"When he did…what? There are laws that protect people like you and Tomas."

"Laws mean nothing to Miguel, Meredith. You don't understand—"

"He's a diplomat, for God's sake, not a hit man. He may have more than a few privileges, but that doesn't mean he can do what he likes."

Julia stepped closer to her friend and dropped her voice. "He's not what you think, Meredith. He has the ability and the power to do anything he wants, and he has a virtual army at his beck and call. He's a dangerous man and—"

She broke off abruptly, her pulse going wild as a

sudden breeze rippled over the garden. Meredith started to speak, but Julia held a finger to her lips and the other woman went silent. Julia exhaled a moment later, the wind brushing past them with a quiet exhalation that matched her own.

Meredith raised an eyebrow.

"I th-thought I smelled Miguel's aftershave." Julia shook her head then rubbed her temples, the rush of adrenaline waking her up to the danger of her indiscretion. What did she think she was doing, telling Meredith these things? If Miguel were to overhear, Julia didn't have to imagine what he'd do. She knew.

Meredith stepped closer and put her hand on Julia's arm. Her breath was warm, her expression concerned. "What can I do to help, Julia? You can't go on like this. There's got to be a way—"

"There's nothing anyone can do. Miguel will never let me go without Tomas and I'm not leaving my son behind."

AFTER THAT Julia said nothing. There was too much at stake for her to be talking like this and she was a fool for sharing what she already had. She shook off the rest of Meredith's questions and the two women went back inside to find the party beginning to break up, a few people already drifting outside to their cars. Standing in the entryway, Miguel was telling everyone good-night, his second in command, Jorge Guillermo, beside him as usual. Half bodyguard, half counselor, he watched Miguel's back as well as his bank account. On occasion, Julia thought she saw sympathy in his eyes when he glanced at her, but deep down, she knew that was only wishful thinking. Guillermo was Miguel's shadow and loyal to a fault.

Both men looked up as Meredith and Julia walked into the living room, and Julia's stomach turned over when Miguel caught her eye. No one else would have seen his displeasure, but she had learned to read the subtleties behind his every expression. He was angry because she'd been in the garden and not at his side.

She walked swiftly to where he waited and began to bid her guests good-night. Meredith was near the end of the line. Miguel extended his hand to Julia's friend, but when she took it, he leaned forward and brushed both her cheeks with a kiss.

"I'm so glad you could come this evening. I know you and Julia had a lot to talk about. I hope she said kind things about me."

Julia held her breath and watched as Meredith smiled warmly at Miguel. "Kind things? She bragged relentlessly and made me envious of her good fortune. Great husband, wonderful home, beautiful child…she has it all. You're both very lucky."

Miguel put his arm around Julia's waist and drew her close. "We make our own luck in San Isidro." He looked at Julia and smiled slowly. "Julia would be the first to tell you that, yes?"

"Of course," she murmured.

Meredith kissed Julia's cheek. "I'll be in touch," she whispered.

As the front door closed behind Meredith, exhaustion swept through Julia. She hid it until the last of the stragglers were gone, then she turned and headed for the stairs to check on Tomas. His bedroom and the nanny's room were on the second floor along with Miguel's office. Miguel's bedroom, just like Julia's, was in a building by itself off a patio on the lower level. She didn't like being separated from Tomas, but Miguel had insisted.

She was halfway up the stairs when Miguel's voice stopped her progress.

"I'd like to see you in my office, Julia. Please change your clothes and meet me there."

She pivoted slowly, her mouth suddenly dry. Had he heard her talking to Meredith? "I'm really tired. Can it wait until tomorrow?"

He seemed to consider her request but both of them knew it was an act. "I'd prefer to discuss this tonight," he said thoughtfully. "The only time I have open tomorrow is when you're supposed to see Tomasito. Would you rather we talk then?"

She fumed but silently. "If those are my choices, then I pick tonight."

He nodded and smiled. "Good."

Thirty minutes later, she was in his office, but Miguel was nowhere to be found. He often made her wait so she wasn't surprised, but his inconsideration bothered her more tonight than usual. She wasn't sure if that was because she'd shared her situation with Meredith or because the headache she'd faked was now becoming real. She crossed his office to stand beside the window and stare at the mountains.

In the valley below, the lights of San Isidro twinkled romantically. When Miguel had brought her to the tiny Colombian village, she'd been enchanted. Quaint streets, red-tiled roofs, charming children… That first day, they'd strolled the twisting sidewalks and Julia had been so happy. She'd thought she'd found true love and was looking forward to starting a family. Everything had seemed so perfect.

A normal woman would have closed her mind to the memories that rose inside her, but Julia no longer considered herself normal. She'd become something else, something that had no name. Miguel had taken away the person she'd been and replaced her with this new being who wanted to remember what had happened because the details fueled her fire.

Closing her eyes, she let the pain roll over her and relished it, the haunting images as fresh now as they'd been four years ago. They'd had a wonderful meal, then Miguel had pulled her into his luxurious bedroom. She'd been looking forward to making love with her husband and she'd moved eagerly into his arms. What had followed was something she *did* blank out.

Stunned and in shock, Julia hadn't known what to do except run. The first time she'd gotten to the gates of the compound. The second time she'd made it to the village. The third time…she couldn't remember how far she made it the third time. Miguel had caught her and locked her in a room somewhere. She still didn't know where it was. He'd kept her there and *visited* until she'd gotten pregnant.

Tomas had been born the following March.

Julia had begged for her freedom.

Miguel's answer had dumbfounded her. "Go ahead," he'd said. "Leave whenever you like."

For a second, she'd let herself think about it, then he'd gotten up from behind his desk and come to where she waited. "If you do go, however, you will go alone. Don't even consider taking Tomasito with you. Should you try, I will hunt you down and bring my son back. I want to raise him here, in San Isidro, to follow in my footsteps."

"But he's my son, too," she'd argued foolishly. "What if I don't want him brought up that way?"

The look in his eyes had been merciless. "What you want or do not want is irrelevant to this discussion. My son will grow up as I desire. You have no say in this matter."

"You can't do that to me," she'd said.

His reply had been simple and irrefutable. "I already have."

Despite the warning, she'd taken Tomas and tried one more time. The punishment for her foolishness had been so painful and humiliating she knew the scars—figuratively and literally—would not disappear. Miguel was a master at abasement and she would never be the same. In the end, though, he'd be the one to pay. Her rage and impotence had had nowhere to go, so she'd turned it inward and forged a determination, the likes of which she'd never felt before.

She *would* escape and she *would* take Tomas with her. Miguel would burn in hell before she'd allow her son to become his father's victim, too.

But explaining all this to Meredith would have been impossible. To begin with, it would have taken more time than they'd had but secondly, Meredith would never have understood how Julia could have gotten herself into this predicament, because Meredith would have never allowed it to happen to herself. Meredith was incredibly strong and assertive and smart. She'd joined the CIA right out of college—the CIA, for goodness' sakes!—then left three years later to start a business with her father, a firm that specialized in international finance. Meredith would have somehow dealt with Miguel and ended the nightmare much sooner. Julia couldn't risk taking her offer of help, though. She'd be damned if she would put anyone else in jeopardy because of her own foolishness.

In the end, it didn't really matter anyway. Julia would rather her friend think she was some kind of helpless idiot than to jeopardize the plans she'd begun to lay.

From behind her, Miguel's voice broke the silence. Her heart pounding painfully, she trembled as she turned.

"Why the shivering? Are you cold? Would you like me to close the window?"

She recovered quickly. "What I would like is to go to bed."

Something shifted in his eyes.

He hadn't touched her since before Tomas's birth, but she worried relentlessly about him coming to her bedroom. She pulled the lapels of the robe she wore closer to her throat.

"Just tell me what you want, Miguel." Her voice stayed steady. "I'm exhausted and my headache is getting worse."

He waited a moment and she held her breath, then he spoke. "I'm leaving town tomorrow. I'll be gone for several weeks and I'm taking Tomasito."

Surprised as she was, she still realized what he'd done. He'd obviously had these plans in place, yet at the party he'd threatened to prevent her from visiting with Tomas. He must really enjoy torturing her.

She hid her anger, the taste of disgust mixing with a flood of fear. There were worse things Miguel could do than toy with her, she reminded herself, and taking Tomas was one of them.

"Where are you going?" The words were hard to get past the knot growing in her throat.

"Where isn't important. All you need to know is that I expect you to remember whose wife you are. You may go into town to visit Portia, if you wish, but not alone."

Portia Lauer was an older woman with whom Julia had developed a friendship. Miguel saw her as harmless and therefore he'd allowed the relationship to continue. His generosity went unnoted; all Julia could think of was her son. "I assume you're taking Mari?"

"No, Mari will not be going. You coddle the boy too much. He can do without his nanny for two weeks."

"Miguel! He's only three—"

"I will handle him."

The words cost her dearly, but Julia said them without reserve. "Then take me with you. I'll watch Tomas for you and you can do whatever it is you need to do."

He seemed to weigh her words, then he dismissed them without even answering, heading for the door instead. At the last minute, he turned. His profile looked like stone in the lamplight. "We're leaving early. If you want to say goodbye, I suggest you keep that in mind."

CHAPTER TWO

JONATHAN CRUZ HAD WORKED with the woman standing in front of him for five years. He felt as if he knew her but now, all at once, he wasn't so sure. Meredith Santera wore an expression he'd never seen on her before.

"It's better than we thought." She paused then appeared to rethink her answer. "Or maybe it's worse," she said. "I guess it depends on your perspective."

"I don't want perspective," he said. "I want the facts."

She walked past the desk where he sitting, toward the couch. The third member of the Operatives team, Armando Torres, sat at one end of it, nursing a beer. There had been a fourth man in their organization, Stratton O'Neil, but he'd left several years ago under terrible circumstances. He'd cleaned himself up and solved his problems, but had chosen not to return, a decision his new wife had helped him make.

His loss had been a tough one. They were a tight group. Meredith and her father, a Navy Intel guy, had started the company and recruited the team right after she'd left the CIA. Cruz had heard all sorts of rumors about why she'd moved on, but he hadn't asked. In their business, questions like that were frowned upon. She assigned the jobs, the team did them and that was that. Their clients came recommended or Meredith wouldn't even talk to them, and the operations were solitary ones, completed with stealth and speed. They had no office and rarely saw one another, but all three of them had happened to be in Bogota at the same time, so they'd met to discuss this job. Cruz had wondered if Meredith had engineered the coincidence, though. The toughest of all of them, she usually made her decisions quickly and acted with confidence, but she was worried about her friend. In a way, her concern made him feel better about her. He'd wondered at times if she had any feelings left.

She kicked off her shoes then took the chair to Cruz's left.

"The facts?" As she repeated his words, her voice was tight and angry with no sign of the drawl she could turn off and on. "The facts are very simple. Miguel Ramirez is a monster. He keeps his wife a virtual hostage by controlling her through their child. He beats her. She hates his guts and would like to see him dead." She took a deep breath and let it out slowly. "But she'll never leave him because, to do that, she'd have to abandon her child. I can guarantee you she won't leave the country that way. Not without her son."

Meredith made a visible effort to control herself. After a moment, she scrubbed her face with her hands, then she looked up at Cruz. "Julia Vandamme is the only friend I have. It killed me to see her tonight. I wanted to stick a blade right into that bastard's black heart then grab her and get the hell out."

"You would have ended up dead, along with your friend."

She blinked, her eyes colder than Cruz had ever seen them. "Maybe, maybe not, but if I hadn't known you guys were waiting for me, that's exactly what I would have done."

Cruz didn't doubt a word of what she said, because Meredith Santera was a killer. Then again, so was Armando. And so was he. Killing was what the Operatives did.

They were assassins and Miguel Ramirez was their next target.

Cruz rose from his desk and walked to the bar. He took out three fresh beers, uncapped them and handed them out. Meredith's was almost empty when he spoke again.

"Tell me more about the setup."

She stared out the window. "The villa's huge. It's made up of one central building that contains everything but the bedrooms, which are in small *casitas* on either side. There are half a dozen smaller buildings scattered around the property and several patios. Needless to say, Ramirez has excellent security.

There are guards around the fenced perimeter and dogs, too. Not to mention electronic sensors—motion, heat, noise detectors. You might get in, but you wouldn't get out."

"What about his people?"

"Very small inner circle. Has one guy who's always close. His name is Jorge Guillermo. Hard to get a handle on him."

Cruz nodded then switched topics. "Do you think she knows who her husband really is?"

Meredith's expression twisted again, this time with such disgust that Cruz knew if he somehow failed to kill the man, the deed would be done regardless by the woman in front of him. For free. And with a cheerful heart.

"You told me what he did to her when she tried to escape. She has to be suspicious at the very least. She told me she knows he isn't a diplomat, but before she could say more, she got spooked."

"Did she say anything about her last attempt?"

"No." Meredith shook her head slowly. "Julia's a very private person and always has been. I was shocked she even told me what she did."

By the time Meredith finished, an hour later, Cruz felt he'd been inside the Ramirez compound himself. Then Meredith looked at him and he knew trouble was coming.

"I know I handed this one over to you, Cruz, but I'm changing my mind. It doesn't make sense for you to go in when I already know the situation. I'm taking this son of a bitch out myself."

"No."

"But Cruz—"

"You gave me the job for a very good reason, Meredith, and that reason hasn't changed in the past twenty-four hours."

"I understand," she said evenly. "But Julia and I have been close for—"

"And that is exactly why you can't do it. Personal involvement is too risky, for you and for the other party."

"'The other party'? She's my friend, Cruz." At her side, Meredith's hands clenched. "If something goes wrong—"

"Nothing will go wrong," Cruz promised. "But you won't be the one doing the job and that's for the best. You and your dad made that rule yourselves and it's a good one."

A stormy expression came into her eyes, but a minute later, her shoulders slumped in defeat. She and her father had made the rules, and she was too smart to let her emotions outweigh common sense.

"All right," she conceded, "but you have to tell me what you're going to do."

"I haven't figured that out yet."

"There's no figuring to it." From the depths of the couch, Armando finally spoke.

His silences could stretch for days, so Cruz wasn't

surprised it'd taken him this long to join the conversation. Cruz looked at the Argentinian physician and raised an eyebrow.

"She gave you the answer already." Armando tilted his beer bottle in Meredith's direction, but his gaze stayed on Cruz. "You don't have enough time to go about this your usual way. Ramirez is going to start his killing in a matter of weeks, maybe even days. When he's done, he'll go underground and you will have an even harder time finding the man. You need to do this one quick."

"What's your point, Armando?" Cruz's impatience was clear, Meredith's attitude making him unusually edgy.

"Let the wife kill him for you."

Meredith was standing before Cruz even saw her move. "No! That's not a possibility, Armando. Julia couldn't handle anything like that."

"But you said—"

"I know what I said. But that's not what I meant. She *can't* kill him—"

"How do you know that?"

"Dammit, Armando, I know, all right? I just know. Julia is different. She's too fragile for that kind of thing—"

"That's enough." Cruz's deep voice cut through the argument. "You've already done what I couldn't and that's get inside tonight. That's all you're going to do, though. This is my job and I'll plan it myself."

TWO HOURS LATER, Cruz was still thinking.

Sitting alone in his dark hotel room, he sipped his Club Colombia and stared at the newspaper article Meredith had left him. His only illumination came from the streetlamp outside the barely parted draperies, but he didn't need more to see the small photo that accompanied the write-up.

Blond hair. Blue eyes. Straight nose. Full lips.

He emptied his beer then let the bottle slide from his fingertips to the floor beside his chair. Cruz knew her type inside and out because he'd seen them in every country he'd ever been in. From the plazas of Mexico City where he'd spent his childhood to the sandy deserts of the Middle East that he'd just left, they turned up. Women who owned the world, that's how he always thought of them. Wealthy, self-confident, gorgeous. Meredith had implied that Julia wasn't that way but Cruz had drawn his own conclusions. From experience.

Women like Julia Vandamme needed men like him to do jobs like this, but those kinds of women seldom allowed his kind of man to get too close. When the deed was done, so were they. Because men like Cruz weren't pliable. And women who owned the world wanted men who did their bidding.

He stared into the darkness and considered his options. Because he was short on time, they weren't as varied as he would have liked, but he'd been successful in tougher situations. Armando's point could not be ignored, however. Miguel Ramirez was the largest drug dealer in Colombia and he was about to launch a bloody war to eliminate his remaining rivals. That roster included half a dozen carefully placed DEA men from the United States who'd been deep undercover for more than five years. They couldn't be pulled or all the progress they'd made would be compromised. But they couldn't be protected, either. Once the shooting started, their positions would be revealed. Getting rid of Ramirez was the only way to take care of the problem *and* keep their Intel network intact.

It was, to say the least, a touchy situation.

Armando's words echoed inside Cruz's head once more. *Let the wife kill him for you.*

Followed by Meredith's fierce rejection of the idea. *Julia is different. She's too fragile for that kind of thing.*

Julia Vandamme had gotten herself into a bad situation that could only get worse, but Meredith didn't suffer fools. For that reason alone, Cruz knew there had to be more to the woman than what he assumed.

Still…

Cruz rose from his chair and parted the curtains to look outside. The lights of Bogota shimmered at his feet as brightly as the stars overhead. Somewhere out there, beyond the mountains that ringed the city, Miguel Ramirez and his beautiful blond wife slept.

They had no idea their lives were about to be shattered.

Cruz stared out at the lights and pondered the best way to do so.

JULIA SET her alarm an hour earlier than usual, but something woke her before it had a chance to ring. Rolling over, she heard the sound again and realized it was a car's engine revving. Immediately suspicious, she jumped from the bed, grabbed her robe and thrust her feet into her slippers. Running to her bedroom door, she jerked it open. The main house was lit up brightly, including the upstairs.

She hurried to the end of the walkway and walked quickly into the entry.

Miguel stood at the bottom of the stairs, holding Tomas in his arms as he spoke with Guillermo. All three of them turned as she came inside, Miguel's surprised expression making it obvious that he hadn't planned on her seeing them before they left.

She felt her whole body go tight with anger. He'd deliberately wanted her to miss saying goodbye to her son. In the beginning, she'd wondered what she'd done to deserve a man like him, but she'd come to realize she'd done nothing—he was simply a cruel son of a bitch.

Tomas began to squirm, but Miguel held on, returning to his conversation with Guillermo. As Julia got closer, however, Tomas took matters into his own hands. Wiggling away, the little boy half jumped, half fell from his father's hold to race toward his mother. Her heart began to swell with love. She *had* to get her son out of San Isidro. He adored Miguel and mimicked everything he did. She couldn't allow that to continue.

She swooped him up and he immediately began to talk excitedly. The words made little sense, except for "airplane" and "dog."

Miguel dismissed Jorge and came to where they stood. Julia started to confront him about the early hour then she checked herself. Showing him how she felt just gave him more satisfaction.

"Tell your mother goodbye." He smiled at his son to reassure him, but beneath the expression, his attitude was cold.

Tomas swung his face to Julia's and gave her a very wet kiss. "Bye-bye, Mama," he said. "I'm going bye-bye!"

She tried to hold on to him, but he escaped her embrace and ran to his father. "Go now, Papa? Go now?"

Somewhere in the middle of the night, Julia had started to worry. What if he didn't bring Tomas back? The question was silly, she knew. Where would he take their son? This was home and Miguel would never leave San Isidro, but the possibility had begun to haunt her.

Despite her earlier stand, she felt herself weaken.

Too much was at stake not to try. "Please tell me where you're going, Miguel." She put her hand on his arm. "I'm his mother. I need to know."

She never touched her husband voluntarily. He looked down at her fingers, pale and slim against his black leather coat, then he raised his eyes to hers. "You're acting foolish. The boy will be with me. Do you think I'd let any harm come to him?"

His words made sense but her anxiety only grew. "Promise me you'll be back in two weeks?"

"Of course, we'll be back. When my business is finished, we'll return." He looked down at Tomas and loosened his grip on the little boy's fingers. "Tell Mama *adios,* Tomasito."

Julia bent down and held out her arms, but Tomas was too fast. Laughing, he darted in and out of her embrace before she could even grab him. He then headed for the front door. With a final look of satisfaction, Miguel followed.

She told herself to stay put, but she couldn't. She ran to the nearest window, the urge to cry overwhelming before the car pulled out of the driveway.

She watched the vehicle until it disappeared, but she didn't allow herself the luxury of tears. Instead, spurred by her fear and last night's conversation with Meredith, she let her long-growing resolve burn just a little bit hotter. She clenched her fists, her arms going tight underneath the silk gown she wore.

She was almost ready. Soon, very soon, she'd try

again. Maybe even when they got back. She had nothing left to lose but her life.

THE NEXT DAY, Cruz waited.

Meredith and even Armando often complained about this part of what they did, but not Cruz. He'd been known to sit quietly, without moving, for hours at a stretch. After a while, the stillness entered his mind as well as his body. And no one knew how much he needed that kind of rest.

But today he would not reach that point. He'd seen the man and the child leave. Julia Vandamme would be on the move soon. She visited only one friend nearby. A woman named Portia Lauer. A British expatriate, the older woman had been friends with Julia for quite some time.

After an hour under the brush halfway up the mountainside opposite Julia's home, Cruz's attention was drawn by a movement at the villa. He peered through his binoculars to see the gates to the compound swing back and a white Toyota Land Cruiser emerge.

As always, there were two people in the vehicle. The sunroof was open and blond hair glittered in the bright morning sun, confirming what he expected. She was in the passenger seat, Guillermo driving.

Crawling from his lair, Cruz took the branches off his motorcycle and started it. In five minutes, he was waiting for them at the first turn. As the SUV reached the incline, the engine whined like a recalcitrant child. Cruz counted down the seconds, then he gunned the bike's motor.

The SUV came into view, and Cruz took off.

A moment later, he drove directly into the vehicle's path and slid beneath its wheels.

GUILLERMO CURSED and Julia screamed. She'd been thinking of Tomas and worrying about him, but she'd gotten a glimpse of the man on the motorcycle before he went down. The sound of the impact was sickening, the screech of metal on metal and the cry of the rubber drowning out every other thought.

Before the Cruiser had stopped, Julia unsnapped her seat belt. Fumbling for the door latch, she was about to climb out when Jorge grabbed her, pulling her back.

"No, no! Stay here," he commanded. "It might be a trap!"

"Are you crazy?" Julia shook off his arm. "It was one man on a motorcycle and he's underneath our car, probably bleeding to death. We've got to see if he's okay!" Without waiting for Jorge's reply, she pushed open the door again and tumbled to the road. She heard him curse again and call her back, but she ignored him.

Falling to her hands and knees, she looked beneath the chassis. Wedged against one wheel, the motorcycle was a tangled mess, the metal handlebars twisted against their front bumper, the leather seat ripped halfway off. She caught her breath, the smell of gasoline and rubber strong as her eyes searched the wreckage. She spotted the driver on the side of the road, his leather pants and jacket torn, blood oozing down his right temple.

Scrambling to her feet, Julia ran to where the man lay. By the time she got there, Jorge had opened his own door and was now standing over him.

Holding a gun.

"Put that away," she cried. "Can't you see he's hurt?" She dropped to the man's side as his eyes fluttered open.

"Are you all right?" Without waiting for his answer, she turned back to Guillermo. He still held the pistol. "Find me the first-aid kit," she said. "It's under the seat in the rear."

Clearly displeased with the turn of events, Guillermo hesitated. "I don't like the way this looks," he said nervously. "Return to the truck and let me call for help. This isn't good—"

"Don't be an idiot," she said from behind clenched teeth. "Go get me the damn kit."

He backed up reluctantly and she focused once more on the injured man.

"Can you hear me?" She couldn't believe he was conscious, much less aware. With no helmet to protect him, she would have expected much worse than the raw scrape on one temple. "Are you okay?"

His gaze flickered to the SUV behind her then fastened on her face. That's when she realized his fingers had formed a handcuff around her wrist. He yanked her closer before she could react.

"Meredith sent me." His voice was a rasp that grated down her spine. "Act like you know me and I'll handle the rest."

CHAPTER THREE

JORGE ROUNDED the fender and the man dropped his hand from her wrist. Blinking in confusion, Julia didn't have enough time to make sense of his words before Jorge was at her side.

"Here." He thrust a small white box in her hands, his eyes narrowing as he stared at the stranger by her feet.

Julia took the first-aid kit numbly. *Meredith had sent this man to help her? Who was he? What could he possibly do? Had he really come from Meredith or was this some new kind of cruel trick Miguel had dreamed up to test Julia?*

She stared at the man and he stared back at her, pushing a strand of his long, brown hair out of his face as he did so. His hazel eyes held a toughness she couldn't ignore, their severity a match to the muscular body his shredded clothing revealed. Because of his body, he looked to be in his twenties, but the resolution in those eyes told her he was much older. Several days' worth of stubble covered his lower jaw and she guessed his last bath had occurred about the same time as his last shave. He seemed poised, as if waiting for her to make the first move, but his look told her she didn't have long.

Afraid something even more dangerous would happen if she stayed quiet, Julia spoke recklessly, spewing out the first thing that came into her mind. "I don't believe this! What on earth are you doing here? My gosh, is this crazy or what—"

The stranger shot her an approving look then he struggled to sit up, extending a hand to Jorge as he did so. "Stan MacDuff," he supplied, looking at Jorge as he spoke. "How ya doing?"

His hands at his side and his gaze never leaving "Stan's," Jorge spoke to Julia. "You know this man?"

"I'm Portia Lauer's nephew from Austin." His drawl became more pronounced as he seemed to mock the bodyguard's concern. "That's in Texas, you know."

"Julia?" Jorge's voice deepened as he said her name, his voice wary.

A wave of unease rolled over her as she glanced at Jorge, who continued, "I asked *you* a question. Do you know this man?"

The biker looked at her, as well. She sealed her fate with three words. "Yes, I do."

Jorge's suspicious expression deepened but, after a heart-pausing moment, he tucked his weapon into his belt and put out his hand. The injured man winced and let out a sharp exhalation as Jorge pulled him to his feet. Julia stood, too.

Ignoring the man's exclamation of surprise, Jorge patted him down with efficient thoroughness. He finished and stepped back, his wariness marginally less visible. Stan winked at Julia before straightening his shirt. "You guys get real friendly around here mighty fast."

"This is a dangerous place." Jorge's reply sounded like a warning instead of an answer. "It is necessary to take precautions."

"That may be true," Stan drawled, "but where I come from, we at least know each other's names when we get that close to someone's *cojones*."

Julia felt as if she should be able to see the tension it was so thick. Her pulse racing, she spoke quickly. "Of course. Where are my manners? Stan, this is an associate of my husband's. Jorge Guillermo."

The two exchanged a handshake as Stan glanced toward the SUV. "Damn, Julia Anne, I'm sorry about your vehicle there. You okay?"

The use of her middle name startled her. He was trying to prove he knew Meredith.

"We're fine." Her voice was a little strained, and she hoped Jorge thought it was caused by shock from the accident. "But I'm not so sure about you. Why don't you let me look at that scrape? It's bleeding pretty badly."

He shook his head. "It's not that serious. We can clean it up at Aunt Portia's. That's where you're heading, right? She told me you were coming over later today. Didn't know I'd run right into you on the way!"

What on earth was happening? How did this total stranger know she was going to Portia's? Julia hadn't told Meredith her plans, had she?

"Portia's is exactly where we were going," she acknowledged. "But are you sure? I think a trip to the clinic might be in order first—"

"No way," he interrupted. "It's nothing but a scratch. Don't think I can say the same for the bike, though."

The three of them looked at the crumpled motorcycle.

"I could probably pull the cycle out from underneath if you could back up the SUV." He turned to Jorge. "What do you think?"

Jorge's expression remained guarded. Miguel surrounded himself with smart people and Jorge was no exception, despite his frequent employment as Julia's babysitter. He and Miguel were as close as brothers and had been ever since soon after they'd met at the University of Texas where they'd both been business majors.

The connection registered immediately. There was no such thing as a coincidence. What did it mean that this man was from Austin, too? Her earlier apprehension returned. What was going on?

Interrupting her thoughts, Jorge handed her the

keys. "Back up the truck," he ordered. "I'll help him remove the motorcycle."

He didn't trust her to be alone with the man—not even for the short time it would take to reverse the SUV. Or was it vice versa? While considering, she hesitated for less than a second, but Jorge noticed regardless.

"Is there a problem?" he asked sharply.

"No," she said. "Absolutely not. I just don't want either of you to get hurt. Is it safe to do this? We could call a wrecker—"

"We'll be fine," the biker said with a slow smile, his eyes locking on hers. "Just fine. Don't you worry."

Once, when she'd been six years old, Julia had left the back door of their Mississippi home open and a rattler had slithered inside. When she'd seen the snake in the kitchen a few minutes later, she'd screamed so loudly the yardman had run into the house without even knocking. He'd compensated for his lapse in protocol by dispatching the unwanted guest.

Since her marriage, she'd often thought she'd let another snake into her life.

Suddenly Julia had the feeling she'd done it again.

THE TWO MEN YANKED the remains of the cycle from beneath the SUV, the Harley's fender screeching a shrill protest against the pavement. They proceeded to gather up the bits and pieces scattered around the road and put them in a pile to one side.

"There's a decent mechanic in town," Guillermo said when they finished. "But I don't know if he's good enough to handle this." He took a handkerchief from his pocket and wiped his hands with it. "He'll need parts from Bogota. If I were you, I'd start looking for another mode of transportation."

The bodyguard's expression was neutral, but Cruz caught the undercurrent of his words. "Good idea," he said in an equally indifferent way. "I'd hate to be stuck here without a way out. Poor planning, you know?"

They exchanged another look, then Julia beeped the horn. Leaning through the open window, she called out. "Are you finished?"

Guillermo nodded and started toward the driver's side of the SUV. Julia got into the passenger seat, and Cruz took the back by himself. Cruz could tell the arrangement made the bodyguard nervous but he held his tongue, started the vehicle and pulled it back onto the road.

"Skip the market," Julia ordered Guillermo, "and go straight to Portia's. We need to get Stan's scrape cleaned up as soon as possible. You can drop us off there then go back and buy the supplies we need."

"That's not how we do it, Julia. Miguel won't like it—"

"It's how we're going to do it today," she replied.

"Because Miguel wouldn't like a lawsuit, either. You were driving way too fast or you would have been able to stop in time." She shot a look over her shoulder at Cruz as if for confirmation. "I'm sure Stan doesn't have plans to raise a fuss but he certainly has grounds to do so."

"The thought never crossed my mind," Cruz answered in a deliberately lazy voice. "I'm not into the justice system myself. I think we oughta dump all the lawyers out to sea and settle our problems ourselves. I bet you agree with that philosophy, huh, Bill?" He reached over the seat and patted Guillermo's shoulder in a friendly way. The touch was brief, but underneath his fingers, he felt the broad strap of a second holster. The body guard had two weapons, just as Cruz expected.

Behind the wheel, Guillermo grunted. Scattering children and dogs, old ladies and chickens, they wound their way through the narrow streets of San Isidro, a cloud of dust marking their passage. There were pockets of privilege and wealth that came close to resembling Miguel's compound with its broadband Internet service and satellite telephones, but most of the city remained in the past. Cruz had been to Havana once and he couldn't help but compare the two places.

There the clock had stopped when Fidel had taken over—the cars were straight from the fifties, few homes had televisions and even fewer had enough food for every member. Here in San Isidro, on the back streets anyway, time had stopped before then. The cars he saw were older and more beat-up and most of the homes had no electricity. Their definition of running water meant it was running in the street, not inside the homes.

They slowed before Portia Lauer's home and Guillermo honked the horn. Under a red-tiled roof, white stucco walls gleamed in the bright sunshine while along the side of the house, rows of bougainvillea swayed in the breeze. In stark contrast to the street they'd just come down, the Englishwoman's villa could have been featured in *Architectural Digest.*

Underneath the beauty, however, the same realities existed. Everyone had to get along and get by. A uniformed guard ran out and opened a set of large metal gates.

Clearly apprehensive, Julia Vandamme turned around in her seat to look at him. "How long have you been staying at Portia's? She didn't tell me she was expecting you."

"She didn't know I was coming. It was a surprise visit," he said. "But I think she was happy to see me." His laugh sounded rusty, even to his ears. "If she wasn't, she put on a good act."

"Portia's always gracious," Julia said, her eyes meeting his. "She's a very special person. I think a lot of your aunt."

Julia Vandamme didn't know what was going on, but her message was obvious. If he had hurt her friend, Cruz could expect some trouble of his own. Although pointless, he was struck by her warning. Just looking at Julia, he would have made the assumption that she wasn't someone who valued loyalty but he'd be mistaken. Maybe that explained her appeal to Meredith. That kind of devotion meant a lot to her.

The SUV pulled to a stop and Guillermo reached for the door handle.

"We'll take it from here," Julia ordered, stopping him with her voice. "There's no need for you to bother."

The bodyguard's jaw twitched and he opened his mouth to protest, but Julia was already out of the vehicle. She slammed the door in his face, then turned to Cruz. He limped pitifully out of the car.

Julia reached out and touched his arm. "Can you walk? Should I go get help?"

"I'm fine," he said stoically. "No problem."

As if realizing what she'd done, Julia snatched her hand away from his arm and sent an uneasy glance toward the SUV. The bodyguard looked at them both then he put the truck in reverse and backed away. Only after the gates had closed, did Julia turn to Cruz.

"You've got ten seconds to explain who the hell you are," she said evenly. "If the story isn't a good one, you're a dead man."

"CAN WE GO INSIDE first?" The man in front of her took a step back and flinched again. "I don't know how much longer my knee is going to hold."

"Did you hurt my friend?" Ignoring his question, Julia tilted her head to the house behind her. "If you hurt Portia—"

"She's fine," he said. "She wants to help you, just like Meredith does. Just like *I* do, if you'll let me."

She stared at him, trying to judge the truth of his answer, but he gave her no more time. Limping, he headed for the front door. Short of screaming for the guard, there was nothing Julia could do but follow. Ever since she'd recovered from her last escape attempt, she'd been working out, but there was no way she could take on this man. He was more than simply tough looking, he really *was* tough and the coldness in those eyes of his told her he wouldn't hesitate to hurt her, either.

He rang the bell then opened the front door and called out. "Aunt Portia, it's me. I'm home."

Before his voice had finished echoing in the marble entry, Portia appeared at the top of the staircase. In her seventies, she'd always seemed like a timeless beauty to Julia, her silver hair shiny, her bearing elegant, her eyes bright. To anyone else, she would have appeared the same now, but Julia saw that she'd aged overnight. Gripping the railing with an unsteady hand, she started down the stairs. "Are you all right, Julia?" she asked.

"I'm fine, Portia." Julia hurried to meet her. "But are you okay?" She took the older woman's arm. "He didn't hurt you, did he?"

"Oh, my goodness, child, no. Nothing's wrong with me. Mr. Cruz is here to help you."

Julia turned to the man who waited below, her eyes narrowing. "*Mr. Cruz?* Is that your real name?"

"Yes, it is." He walked to where Julia and Portia waited, his limp gone. "My name is Jonathan Cruz and before you can ask again, yes, Meredith *did* send me." His expression shifted slightly. "She said to tell you I'm a *bueno gib,* whatever in the hell that means."

Julia kept her face neutral but with those two words, Meredith authenticated Jonathan Cruz in a way that left no confusion. She and Julia had made up the code words in college for guys they thought would be really good in bed. Using the term now for another reason, Meredith knew this would be the best way for Cruz to gain Julia's trust. No one but the two of them even knew the foolish phrase.

Still, she hesitated. "Why would Meredith send you? If she wants to help me, why didn't she come herself?"

"Let's just say I have some special skills that Meredith doesn't. We thought this would be the best way."

Julia felt her pulse begin to race. Jonathan Cruz had already scared her, but now he was making her worried. "I don't think I believe you." She started to walk away from him. "I'm calling Meredith right now—"

He stepped to her side and stopped her, his fingers gripping her arm. "No phone calls. The lines are bugged."

In reflex, Julia's startled eyes met his.

"You're just going to have to believe me," he said. "After she saw how things were at the party, she wanted to do something to help you. She said she couldn't stand by and let your husband ruin the rest of your life. She really did send me."

"Well, if she did, she made a mistake." Julia started to add more, then she stopped. Meredith didn't know who she was dealing with—Miguel was ruthless. The only law he respected was his own and if she got in his way, Miguel wouldn't hesitate to remove her.

"I'm sorry you went to so much trouble, but you can turn around and go back from wherever you came. I don't need Meredith's interference." Still wary despite the code word, she kept her own plans to herself, only adding, "It'll just make things more complicated. If Meredith did send you, then she'll understand why your presence here isn't helpful."

"I've been given a job to do and until that job is done, I can't leave San Isidro."

"I appreciate the thought, but I take care of my own problems," she replied icily. "I don't want to be rescued."

"That sounds good." His drawl disappeared, along with his injury, and he spoke in a way that matched his hard, cold eyes. "But you're going to think differently once you get in the jungle and your husband comes after you. You can't just run away and expect a man like Miguel Ramirez not to react. He'll come after you and won't stop until the day he dies. I'm here to make sure that day arrives sooner than he'd like." He stared at her flatly. "I'm going to kill your husband and you're going to help me do it."

Suddenly she felt as if her life had turned into a bad movie and all Julie could do was stutter. "Wh-wh…?"

Moving closer to the bottom stair, he repeated himself as if she'd asked him for the time of day. "I said I'm going to kill your husband. And you're going to help."

Julia turned in a daze and stared at Portia.

The older woman clutched Julia's arm. "Come and sit down, Julia. I think you need to hear what Señor Cruz has to say."

She let herself be led into the living room. The area was huge and it merged seamlessly with the patio outside. There were French doors between the two, but Julia had never seen them closed. At one end of the vast space, Portia kept cages filled with wild canaries. The birds were singing when they entered the room, their colorful wings flashing, their sweet voices mingling with the sound of the wind chimes

Portia collected. There were dozens of them dangling outside, in the trees, on the patio, off the overhang of the roof.

Refusing the older woman's urging to sit, Julia stood beside one of the couches in a state of shock. Jonathan Cruz took off his jacket and dropped it onto a nearby chair, then he walked to the unlit fireplace.

"I'm going to get tea," Portia said. She gave the unshaven man a look that Julia wasn't able to interpret, then left the room. Chita, Portia's maid, scurried in with a basin of water, clean towels and antiseptic ointment. She dabbed at Jonathan Cruz's face with an efficiency that said she'd done this sort of thing before. When she reached for the bandages, though, he shook his head.

She left and the birds continued to sing, but this time their songs were more subdued, as if they felt the tension in the air.

"Explain yourself," Julia said to the man.

"You've gotten all the information you're going to get," he said. "The only question that remains is whether or not you'll help me or get in my way."

"Do you actually know Meredith or did she just give you the words to use?"

"I know her."

"How?"

"That isn't important."

"It is to me."

He made no further comment and Julia's mind

spun. Meredith had refused to say anything about her
time at the CIA, but Julia knew it had ended on a sour
note about a year after she'd married. Meredith and
her father had started their company after that. Had
Julia met Jonathan Cruz at the CIA? Had she really
hired him to do this?

"*If,* and that's a huge if," she said finally, "you're
telling me the truth, why on earth would Meredith
want to kill Miguel?"

"She's trying to save your life."

"I can do that myself."

"Maybe so, but having some help wouldn't hurt
and she knows that. There's always a need for people like me. Sometimes it's the only solution."

Julia could hardly speak. "Are you telling me
Meredith *paid* you to come down here? That you're
some kind of…hit man or something?"

Instead of answering, he walked over to her. She
wanted to back away from him, but she stood her
ground. His eyes held flecks of gold as well as green
and for the first time, she saw his scar. A long thin
line ran from his right ear all the way down his neck
before disappearing beneath his shirt.

"Meredith told me she wasn't sure you knew who
your husband really is, but I think you do. I think you
must also know that you won't survive once you
leave here unless Miguel Ramirez is dead. You might
get out of the jungle, hell, you might even get out of
the country but if you do, you'll spend the rest of

your life looking over your shoulder because you know—" he stopped for emphasis and repeated himself "—*you know* that you can't take away his son and expect him to just forget about it."

"I understand the dynamics of my situation, Mr. Cruz. I don't need you to explain them to me."

"How do you intend to handle the problem?"

She felt herself flush. "I have to get out of here first. Then I'll deal with Miguel."

He shook his head. "You've got it backward. First you've got to deal *with* Miguel, and then you can get out of here. If you don't, you're going to end up dead. Maybe when you least expect it."

He'd said nothing that she hadn't thought of already, but Julia suddenly felt sick. She'd been too short-sighted. Again. His bluntness lifted the blindness that her determination had masked. Miguel would come after her. Forever. Or until he had Tomas back.

But *kill* him? Just like that? Could she stand by and let that happen?

She looked at Cruz. "You're really serious, aren't you?"

"Do I look like a man who kids?"

They both knew the answer to that question, but Julia was the one who spoke. "No, you don't," she admitted, "but you don't look crazy, either. You have to be, though, if you think you can harm Miguel. We live in a fortress with too many bodyguards to count.

He has weapons close by at all times. He keeps me and my son virtual prisoners. No one can get to Miguel."

"I got to you," he said with confidence. "I can get to him, too."

He spoke with such assurance that she couldn't help herself. She thought of what it would mean if he could really do what he was proposing.

She'd be free. Free to live her life again. No more endless questions about her activities. No keeping quiet when she wanted to scream. No more fear for Tomas and his future.

The thought of her son brought her back to earth with a crash. Help would be great, but the freedom she sought for herself and Tomas was too important to leave in the hands of a stranger. She'd trusted Miguel and look where that had gotten her.

"You're nuts," she said bluntly. "I'm not helping you do anything, much less kill Miguel."

UNDER HIS BREATH, Cruz cursed Meredith. And then he cursed himself. He'd let her persuade him that the direct approach would be the one to use with Julia Vandamme. He should have done the job like he always did. On his own. Quietly. Simply.

Normally, Meredith wouldn't have convinced him to go against his better judgment, but time was short. Armando had been right. Julia had become a short-cut Cruz *had* to take.

It didn't matter, though. What was done, was done. Julia Vandamme knew the truth now, so he had to proceed the best way he could.

"You no longer have a choice in the matter," he said. "If you don't see things my way, I can pretty well guarantee you'll be arrested for Miguel Ramirez's murder. He *is* going to die and you'll be the only one left for the *policia* to blame."

She seemed to blanch, but it was hard to tell. Her ivory skin had lost most of its color at the start of their conversation.

"That sounds like a threat," she said softly.

"It's called the truth from where I stand," he replied. "But the results are going to be the same regardless of what we call it. I'm going to come into your house and kill your husband. Unless you agree to help me out, you won't know when and you won't know how. You'll be in the dark until the local uniforms arrive, find his body and throw your ass in jail. That will be the last anyone will ever hear about you." He moved a step closer to her. "Unless you choose the alternative."

"Which is?"

"Do what I ask when the time is right."

"And in return?"

"I'll help you and your son get out of the country."

She licked her lips nervously, pulling his gaze to her mouth. "Meredith is my friend. She'd *never* put me or Tomas in danger like that. She'd get us out first."

"Maybe so," he answered harshly. "But Meredith isn't here. I am. And I'm going to do this my way. All you have to decide is if you want to help me and escape, or if you want to stick around and gamble with your future. I'm very good at what I do, Mrs. Ramirez. You'd better think hard before you make your decision, because once it's been made, there's no going back. For any of us."

"I hate Miguel, but killing him?" Her throat moved as she swallowed. "Murder is something entirely different."

"That's not what you told Meredith. You said you'd kill him yourself if you could."

"I did say that," she conceded. "But in the heat of the moment we've all said things that might have been better left unsaid. Surely, you're guilty yourself of what I'm talking about, Mr. Cruz."

"Actually, I'm not. When I say I'm going to do something, it gets done."

She looked at him, their impasse building, until he reached out and took a strand of her hair. Winding it around his finger, he dropped his voice. "I've heard the jail over in Cali is a pretty rough place but *las rubias* go over big everywhere. You're pretty and young, thin and blond. You'd probably be able to cut some kind of deal along the way, but you'll never see your kid again."

CHAPTER FOUR

INCHES AWAY from Cruz, Julia tugged her hair away from his grip, then stepped back. "What kind of bastard are you?" she whispered, his words taking away her ability to speak normally.

"One who's been hired to do a job," he said. "Which I intend to complete, whether you participate or not." Pivoting, he picked up his leather jacket, slipping his arms into the sleeves as he walked toward the front door. "I'll give you two days, then I have to have my answer."

"Two days? But Miguel's gone," she protested. "I can't—"

"What do you mean 'gone'?"

"He took Tomas and left this morning. He said they'd be gone two weeks."

"Where'd they go?"

"I have no idea. He wouldn't tell me."

His jaw went tight. "Try harder."

"I'm telling you the truth!" she cried. "I don't have a clue where they went."

A small silence built, then he spoke again. "Well,

he'll come back sooner or later. It'd be best to have our plans in place regardless. You've got two days."

"But I need more time to make a decision like this! You can't possibly do anything that quickly anyway."

He slowly came back to where she waited. Her heart thrummed in response, every resource she had telling her to flee the danger he represented. She told herself she was being silly, but she thought that she could actually *feel* his energy as he drew near. He seemed to vibrate with an intensity that was barely contained.

"I can do anything I want to and I can do it at any time." His voice was low and strangely pleasant. "You wouldn't see me, you wouldn't hear me, you wouldn't have a clue that I had even been there. I'll leave a body behind and that's the only way you'll know I was there."

He lifted her chin with his thumb, forcing her to look at his face. An icy paralysis kept her from moving.

"There are probably worse things you could do than underestimate me, but I wouldn't suggest you try it. You'll end up very unhappy, I promise."

She blinked then bluffed. "I'm living in hell right now. There's nothing you could do to me to make my life any worse."

"Are you sure of that?"

She opened her mouth to say yes then thought again.

Reading her hesitation as if she'd spoken it, he smiled coldly. "You look like a smart woman. Make the right decision and you'll stay alive as well."

He dropped his fingers and walked out the front door.

An hour later, despite Portia's tea and explanations, Julia was still trembling. They'd covered everything, including Miguel's disappearance with Tomas, but the conversation kept returning to Jonathan Cruz.

"I had to help him, Julia, please understand. He didn't give me a choice in the matter."

They were outdoors on Portia's patio. Aided by the warm sun overhead and the carefully cultivated serenity of the garden, the older woman had recovered her composure, but Julia wasn't sure she would ever regain hers. Hearing her teacup rattle against its saucer, she made a sound of disgust and put the china down on the table before her. After all Miguel had put Julia though, she would have thought she could have handled the situation better. She was shocked at how deeply Jonathan Cruz had managed to upset her.

Portia reached over and took Julia's cold fingers. "Please don't be angry with me."

"Oh, Portia, I could never be angry with you." Julia squeezed her friend's fingers before letting them go. "I'm just confused and scared. Who *is* Jonathan Cruz? Could Meredith have really sent him here to kill Miguel?"

"He told you more than he told me, sweetheart. I know nothing else."

Portia's voice trembled and Julia said in sympathy, "He used you to get to me. I'm sorry."

"You have nothing to apologize for," she said. "And I didn't mind because I love you and want the best for you." Her blue eyes turned brighter in the sunshine. "Face the truth, Julia. With this man's assistance, you might be able to leave."

In Portia's voice, Julia heard the hope the older woman no longer had for herself. She and her husband had come to San Isidro as part of a mission over thirty years before. When her husband had passed away two years ago, she'd gone back to London, but a month later, she'd returned to Colombia saying London was too cold and rainy. But Julia had understood the real reason. There was nothing in the U.K. for her anymore. The village had become her home; she could live here cheaply and her friends were nearby.

Her fear combining with her frustration, she pushed her chair back and stood. The muffled sound of a passing delivery truck slipped over the garden wall. When the noise died, Julia spoke flatly. "I don't like him," she said. "There's something about Jonathan Cruz that's not right."

"But he can help you."

"I could be better off on my own. Something tells me his aid will be costly."

"What do you mean?"

"I'm not sure," Julia said thoughtfully. "I just have the gut feeling that there's more going on here than I know about."

"Are you sure you don't want to try to call your friend?"

"It's just too risky. He said the phones could be bugged and he's right." Meredith might have developed skills and met killers at the CIA, but Julia was afraid her friend had no idea what she was getting into when she crossed Miguel. Julia couldn't warn her, either, or the danger would increase for both of them. "I know they're wired at home. I'm going to have to decide what to do on my own."

"You'll make the right choice."

Julia wished she shared Portia's confidence. "What if it's a trap? What if he isn't who he says he is? What if I trust him then something goes wrong?"

"You're not asking yourself the real question." Portia stood then rested her hands on the back of her chair, her silver hair shining in the bright light.

"And that is?"

"What if you *don't* trust him and he proves to be your only hope?"

RETURNING TO the ratty hotel on the edge of town where he was staying, Cruz found a coded message waiting for him. Translating the note from Meredith, he cursed. Ramirez was moving faster than they'd anticipated, arranging meetings and setting plans, all in preparation to eliminate his competitors. Ramirez's trip had to be a part of that, but if it was, why had he taken the kid? Dammit! The window of opportunity was narrowing fast and complications like this didn't help things. How could he put his plan into motion if he didn't even know where in the hell Ramirez was?

Throwing his backpack to the bed, he retrieved the expensive electronics he'd hidden before he'd left. He hadn't lied to Julia about the listening devices he'd discovered. The house itself had not been bugged but he'd found several wiretaps. He'd left them in place and added his equipment to the mix. Portia's house had been clean, though. It'd been a simple thing to hide his devices the first time he'd been there.

He grabbed his earphones and adjusted the volumes. The recorded voices of the older woman and of Julia were so clear, he felt as if he were still standing in the room with them.

He listened to the entire conversation, then let it play again. When it finished the second time, he ripped off his headphones, his uneasiness growing. It didn't bother him that Julia Vandamme didn't care for him, but he was in trouble if she hadn't bought the story that Meredith had hired him. Without her cooperation he could get the task done, but with it, things would go much smoother. The lives of too many good men rested on Cruz's shoulders for him to ignore the urgency that was building.

He walked to the window to stare outside, his thoughts returning to Julia Vandamme. Because he'd been watching her through the binoculars for a couple of days, he'd known what to expect and he didn't have to wonder what she'd thought of his unkempt hair, his cheap jeans or his unshaven jaw. Along with the disgust, he'd seen the fear and suspicion in her eyes. He'd noted the reaction with his usual detachment but the more he thought about it, the more confused he became, especially after listening to the two women talk.

Julia was from a different world than Miguel Ramirez was, but the only difference between Cruz and Ramirez was that the Colombian knew how to camouflage his background and Cruz didn't bother. They were both users of people who lived outside the boundaries of the regular world. The similarities he'd begun to notice between himself and Julia's husband had not been surprising to Cruz. He'd often felt a deeper affinity for his target than for those who paid his fee but he'd never been bothered by that.

Until now.

He frowned then went back to the bed and started the recorder again. Freed from the earphones he'd been using, Julia's elegant tones rang out, completely incongruent within the sleazy room in which he stood.

I don't like him. There's something about

Jonathan Cruz that's not right.... I just have the gut feeling that there's more going on here...

Julia Vandamme *looked* like a rich socialite, but she didn't act like one. Behind the smooth blond hair and bright blue eyes there was an attitude that didn't match his expectations. In fact, he realized slowly, her facade covered the exact kind of determination and resolution that Meredith had. And Meredith was a killer.

He shut off the recorder, Julia's words now etched in his mind as surely as if he'd voiced them himself.

Her instincts were good, he decided, very good. Surprisingly good. Dangerously good.

He might be in trouble in more ways than he expected.

EXCEPT FOR A PASSING NAP, Julia didn't sleep for forty-eight hours. When the third day came and went and she'd heard nothing further from Cruz, she thought she might lose her mind. He'd said she had two days, so where was he? What was happening? She gave up and took half of a sleeping pill, falling into a state too restless to be called sleep yet too deep to be called anything else.

Despite her exhaustion and the medication, when the lights in her bedroom flashed on at 3:00 a.m., she opened her eyes to immediate awareness.

Halfway anticipating Cruz, she sat up in the bed

and blinked in surprise. Her husband stood in the center of the room.

"Miguel!" She spoke his name almost guiltily. "You're back! I wasn't expecting you! Is Tomas in his room?" She threw off her tangled bed linens. "I want to see him—"

Miguel walked slowly to the edge of the bed, his expression freezing her in place. "You want to see someone, I'm sure, but I do not think it is your son you are missing."

She drew in her breath so sharply he heard her.

"Don't bother to act surprised," he said coldly. "I know what you've been doing."

As if a giant fist had reached inside her chest and squeezed it, her heart felt tight. Guillermo must have called and told Miguel about the incident with Cruz. Suspicious and paranoid already, Miguel had let his jealousy take flight.

"I don't know what you're talking about," she answered. "I wasn't expecting you, much less anyone else. What kind of craziness have you dreamed up now?"

He tossed something onto the bed. Whatever it was, it landed lightly and she had to dig through the sheets until a flash of black caught her eye. Her fingers trembling, she picked up the book of matches. They were from a club, a club in Austin, Texas. Across a glossy black background, The Yellow Rose was spelled out in gold script letters. The outline of a nude woman could be seen behind the flower. Her stomach flipped over. She had no idea how he'd done it, but Jonathan Cruz must have had a hand in this. Had he planted the matches so Miguel would find them? But why? And how?

She looked up at Miguel, suddenly grateful that she hadn't gotten out of bed after all. She wasn't sure her legs would have held her. "Where did these come from?" she asked.

"Funny you should ask. That's my very question for you," he said. "I found them inside your purse. Perhaps you could tell me then we'll both know."

She dropped the matchbook and got out of the bed, reaching for her robe. Wrapping it around her, she spoke calmly. "I have no idea where they came from, Miguel. I didn't make a two-day trip to Austin and fly back while you were gone, if that's what you're worried about."

He took a step toward her and she flinched. He hadn't actually hit her in quite some time, but some old habits couldn't be broken.

"Tell me where you got those matches," he growled. "Or I swear to God you'll never see your son again."

Her throat closed up, but she wouldn't let him see her fear—it would please him too much and feed his suspicion as well. Instead, she concentrated on figuring out exactly what Guillermo could have told him. She made her decision quickly.

"I probably picked them up at Portia's," she said tying her robe. "Her nephew was here the other day and he's from Austin. The three of us sat outside in Portia's garden and visited. She had candles lit. I must have taken them by accident."

Miguel's fierce expression didn't waver, but Julia caught the subtle shift. His shoulders seemed to ease and she could see he'd begun to accept her answer, albeit reluctantly. Her pulse still in a turmoil, she tried to change the subject. "Where's Tomas? I want to see him—"

"I'm not staying. I didn't bring him with me."

She stared at Miguel dumbly. "What do you mean, you didn't bring him? Where is he? Who's taking care of him—"

"Tomas is safe," Miguel interrupted. "That's all you need to know."

His words reminded her of Cruz's threat and suddenly she was tired of men telling her only what they thought she *needed* to know.

"I want to know where he is, Miguel. What have you done with my son?"

"I'm going to check out your story, Julia. If you've lied to me, you're in serious trouble."

She ignored his attempt at intimidation just as he ignored her questions. "Please, Miguel! Please tell me where Tomas is—"

Without saying a word, he stepped outside and closed the door behind him. Julia started after him with a muttered curse, then halfway across her bedroom she stopped. Confronting Miguel would gain her nothing, except possibly a black eye.

Swallowing her pride and choking back her concern for her baby, she turned away, her anger shifting into a resolve that would serve her much better. She *would* escape San Isidro and she *would* take her son with her. She'd do it by herself, too.

Picking up the book of matches from her bed, Julia tightened her fingers around it until the edges cut into the flesh of her palm, the pain a welcome reinforcement to her decision.

She didn't know why Jonathan Cruz had come to her, but one thing was for certain; he wasn't there to help her. The matches proved that.

WHEN SHE WOKE UP the following morning, the first thing Julia did was check with the housekeeper. Just as he'd said, Miguel hadn't stayed. In fact, he hadn't even spent the night. She let out a sigh of relief and then thought about her second concern—why hadn't Cruz contacted her? Had Miguel done something to him? She worried most of the morning then she decided to focus on her escape plans. With a renewed sense of purpose, she headed to the gym Miguel had had installed inside the compound just for her.

She'd been surprised by his generosity until she'd come to understand. He indulged her interest in working out because he didn't want her to put on weight. Inside his twisted mind, he'd decided that having her look good made him look good. To him, she was a status symbol. Like his cars and boats, he wanted her to be sleek and sexy. A possession to be envied.

What he failed to notice was that she was also becoming strong and hard.

For two solid hours, she lifted weights and pounded the treadmill. Every step she ran, every barbell she hefted, took her a little bit closer to freedom. The last time she'd tried to run away, she'd made the mistake of thinking her desire to escape was enough to overcome her limitations. She'd learned better. When she made her next move, she'd be in top physical condition, able to protect herself and her boy. Neither the jungle nor Miguel's goons would have a chance against her.

Returning to her room, she cleaned up, ate some fresh mango, then called Portia. They met once a week at the Intercontinental Hotel. As tiny as San Isidro was, the town had its fair share of nice hotels and restaurants to service the tourists, most of whom came in from Cali. Built in the 1700s, the local cathedral provided the main attraction, but the beautiful scenery also drew them. The majority of homes might not have indoor plumbing, but the hotel had a swimming pool that was heated and cooled and their spa featured mud baths from the ruins nearby.

They hadn't spoken since Julia had left Portia's home, but they'd arranged a code just in case.

"It's me," Julia said when Portia answered. "Are you on for our girl's day out or is the painter still working in the kitchen?"

"I haven't seen him again so I guess he's finished," Portia replied. Julia made the translation quickly: Cruz had not returned to Portia's since their original visit.

The news should have made Julia relax, but for some reason it had the opposite effect. She questioned her reaction then decided the answer was simple. As long as she could predict what someone might do, she could be prepared, but Cruz wasn't the kind of man who telegraphed his intentions. He certainly hadn't contacted her within the time he said he would. The unfamiliar and unpredictable had always bothered her, especially since her one and only impulsive act had led to the disaster she was now living.

Leaving the compound didn't seem like such a good idea now. "Well, I was calling to see if you might like to go into town, but if another day would be better, I wouldn't mind. I'm sure you need to clean up whatever mess the workmen left."

Portia disappointed her. "No, no. Chita can take care of it. I'd really like to keep our appointment at the spa, if you can go, too."

"Of course," Julia answered, covering her reluctance. "I'll see you at the hotel at four."

Returning to the small office she'd made for herself off her bedroom, Julia locked her door then pulled out the maps she kept hidden. She'd gotten lost last time she'd tried to run, but that wasn't going to happen again. She was plotting her course much more carefully, memorizing her primary route and two backups. Totally engrossed in her work, she looked up to see two hours had passed. Hiding her things once more, she left her bedroom and made her way to the garage where Guillermo was already waiting.

She climbed inside the Toyota and he started for the gate. They usually spoke very little and, even though Julia would have liked to ask him if he'd been the one to tell Miguel about Cruz, she knew it would be best to maintain her normal silence.

Guillermo surprised her by bringing up the subject himself. "Have you spoken with Portia?" he asked. "I was wondering if her nephew got his motorcycle fixed."

Julia looked out the window on her right as if the subject bored her. "We spoke," she said carelessly, "but she didn't mention anything about the motorcycle."

Guillermo said nothing more until they arrived at the hotel. "Tell Portia I'd be happy to help her *sobrino* if he needs any assistance." His eyes met Julia's. "Miguel told me to make sure he has transportation."

His words made breathing difficult. She spoke calmly, though. "I'll pass on the message."

"Bueno," he answered. "I will park then wait for you in the lobby."

Climbing from the SUV, she entered the elegant hotel, her mouth dry with fear. Miguel had obviously checked Cruz out and believed the man to be Portia's nephew; otherwise, he'd be dead. The warning was clear, despite that fact, however. Miguel wanted Cruz gone and gone quickly.

Crossing the marbled lobby, Julia composed herself, keeping her head high and her face blank. Miguel had spies everywhere and they reported the smallest thing, even down to her expressions. She didn't want to give him anything else to think about. The matches had been enough to trigger the warning.

Her footsteps fell silent as she headed down the plush-carpeted hallway that led to the spa. Opening the beveled glass doors, she barely had time to greet Portia and tell her of Miguel's visit and Guillermo's threat before the masseuse came out to retrieve them for their respective treatments.

"I'll explain everything after we've finished," Julia promised the older woman.

Portia nodded and then went in the opposite direction. She looked frailer than she had on Monday, Julia thought with some alarm. Was Cruz bothering her or had something else come up? Maybe he'd been in her house when Julia had called, and the older woman hadn't been able to tell Julia. She started to go after Portia, but at the last minute, she managed to convince herself she was acting crazy. If anything more had happened, Portia could have told her. Julia was letting her fears get to her.

The masseuse opened the door to her suite, showed Julia in, then stepped back out. The room was designed to soothe the worst stress with low lights and soft colors, padded walls and quiet music. Julia continued to worry about her friend, however, as she disrobed then climbed onto the table, slipping under the sheet stretched over it.

The door opened a few minutes later then closed softly. The masseuse had returned. Julia waited patiently for the woman to begin, but the room stayed silent and still. She was just about to turn her head when a pair of warm, oiled hands reached for her shoulders.

Strong fingers immediately began to knead Julia's muscles, starting out slow but magically finding the spots where she was the tightest. She closed her eyes as the sensual rhythm built, then all at once the movement stopped.

"Por favor, el momento..."

Julia frowned and looked back, but the woman had already slipped out the door.

A second later, Jonathan Cruz stepped in.

CHAPTER FIVE

BENEATH THE DESIGNER clothes and salon-styled hair, Julia Vandamme had an unexpectedly lean and muscular body. Another contradiction, Cruz thought.

Her startled eyes met his and instantly reminded him of the small feral cats he'd seen in the jungles of Borneo, their sleek fur shining in the dappled foliage, their spots blending so perfectly they stayed invisible to all but the keenest of observers. They liked to hide in the trees, he remembered, and pounce from above to kill their unsuspecting prey.

She lay motionless on the table for another second, then she pulled the sheet up higher and stared at him without speaking.

"Your masseuse got called away. A family emergency, I believe." He let his eyes dip to the curve of her breasts. "I'd be happy to finish for her if you like."

Tucking the sheet closer to her body, Julia sat up, ignoring his offer. "Where have you been? I thought you said two days and it's been—"

"I had things to do." He hardened his stare as he

interrupted her. Things like keeping her on edge and off balance. He'd deliberately postponed calling her to raise her level of nervousness. The tactic looked as if it had worked.

"Well, in the meantime, Miguel found the matches you planted in my purse. What are you trying to do? Get me killed?"

He frowned. "What matches?"

"The ones from The Yellow Rose in Austin." Shaking her head, she looked at him in disgust. "I know you put them there so don't bother denying it. Are you thinking you can blackmail me or something?"

"I don't know what you're talking about," he answered. "But if you found something in your purse from Austin, I didn't put it there. The only other person who knows I'm 'from' there is Jorge. Why don't you ask him?"

She frowned. "Why would he do something like that?"

Cruz waited a beat. "You really don't get it, do you?"

Her mouth went tight. "Get what?"

"You live in a bad place, Julia. Figuratively and literally. Everyone in San Isidro looks out for themselves first, and no one else second. Anyone with any influence on Miguel is competition with Jorge. And he's not the kind of guy who wants help, if you know what I mean."

"I have no power over Miguel," she said bitterly. "I have no power, period."

Cruz shrugged. "He might not know that. Or he might not care. You complicate things. Anything he can do to make you look bad in Miguel's eyes would probably help him. I'd guess he just wanted to throw something into the mix." He paused, then went on. "It doesn't matter. Are you going to help me or have you decided to stay in San Isidro and spend the rest of your life as Miguel Ramirez's slave?"

She obviously wanted to pursue the issue of the matches, but his words successfully distracted her. "I don't intend to do either."

"You can't get away on your own." He pushed himself away from the wall and passed by a ledge that was filled with candles. Rising ribbons of light and heat filled the shadowy room, along with the scent of plumeria. "I know what happened to you last time."

"How do you know that?"

"I make it a point to find out what I'm getting into before I get into it."

His words hit home just as he'd planned. "Well, you may *think* you know," she said, "but you don't. Experiencing the actual event gives you a unique perspective."

He reached up and touched his neck without thinking, the thin scar a ridge beneath his fingers. "You make an excellent point."

"I'm glad you understand." She swung her legs off the table and eased down, the sheet trailing behind her. "Because that makes it easier for you to accept the fact that I can't help you. I'll handle my own problem."

"And Miguel?"

Her voice was cold. "What about him?"

"What are you going to do when he shows up in Pascagoula?"

Her face paled. "Who says I'm going there?"

He held her gaze without answering and walked around the massage table to the small chair in the corner of the room. She'd piled her clothing on it and he reached down and picked her things up, piece by piece. Holding them loosely, Cruz sat down, crossed his ankle over his knee and dropped the garments into his lap. "You're no match for Miguel Ramirez. You don't know what you're doing and you're going to get yourself killed," he said pleasantly. "Where's that going to leave your son?"

"Give me my clothes."

"You don't need them." His eyes went to the sheet then back up to her stony face. "I can't see anything."

"I want to get dressed and I want to get out of here. Hand them over."

"I will," he replied, "but you should listen to me first. You'll thank me later."

"I doubt that." Her anger was growing, but calling for help was not an option and she couldn't take him on alone. "But I don't have much of a choice, do I? Once again, you've arranged things to your liking."

"That's how I operate," Cruz said flatly. "Life is simpler that way."

"For you," she retorted.

"For everyone."

She lifted the end of the sheet off the floor then walked to the other side of the table, putting as much distance as she could between them.

"Start talking," she said tersely. "I'll give you five minutes."

He didn't waste time arguing for more. "You and I both know what your husband does so I'm going to be blunt," Cruz began. "He's in a dangerous business with a lot of competition. In an effort to consolidate his power, he's making plans to see that some of that competition disappears." He paused. "Permanently. When that happens, you don't want to be around here."

She put a hand to the base of her throat. "How do you know this? Is that why Meredith—"

"Not important," he interrupted her question. "You need to get out of San Isidro before the killing begins. If you wait, you'll never make it."

"When is this going to start?"

"Your husband hasn't shared his timetable with me but I'd say soon. Most likely in less time than you need to do whatever it is you think you're going to do."

"You can't possibly know that for sure—"

"Yes, I do. And you would, too," he said, "if you had the whole story."

"I do have the whole story," she said, her expression bitter. "I have more of it than I ever wanted to have, believe me."

"Is that so?" His impatience growing, Cruz didn't wait for an answer. "Do you know he arranged to meet you? That he picked *you*. Do you know where Tomas is right now?"

He could see his questions were not new to Julia. She'd clearly given a great deal of thought to each of them, but only one really mattered. Taking an unconscious step toward him at the mention of her son's name, she sucked in her breath, her words rushing out as she exhaled. "You know where Tomas is? Is he safe? Is he really all right—"

Her reaction stirred an emotion so deeply buried inside Cruz it took him a second to remember it was called sympathy. In his line of work, feelings were best forgotten.

"I can't say exactly where he is, but I do know he is safe."

"Oh, my God! How did you get this information? Are you sure—"

"He's safe," Cruz repeated, "but for how long? It's not a secret that your husband wants him in the family business and it's not one known for longevity."

"I'm getting Tomas out of here before that happens."

"You may be too late," Cruz said. "Ramirez has taken the first steps to see that his wishes are carried out. That's why he took the boy and left." Cruz paused. "He's going to give your child to his mistress and she's going to raise him just as Miguel wants."

CRUZ COULD HAVE THROWN a right hook to her jaw and Julia would have felt no different. A mixture of disbelief and horror stunned her, making her break out in a cold sweat. She opened her mouth, but no words came out.

She'd long suspected Miguel had another woman, but the rest of Cruz's allegation, if it were true, was simply unbelievable. Someone else raise Tomas? The very idea was preposterous.

Cruz rose, dropped her clothes on the table and walked around the end of it to where she stood.

She held out her palm and stopped him before he got too near, her voice finally returning. "What are you talking about? Tomas is my son."

Brushing aside her arm, Cruz came closer and rested his hands on her bare shoulders as if to steady her. If she'd been thinking, she would been shocked by the pity in his touch, but she was too overwhelmed by his news for anything else to register.

"Miguel has a lover named Amalia Riveria. She's in the business with him."

"I thought he might have a mistress," she said faintly. "But the other, I can't believe."

"Amalia Riveria was with him before he ever married you and she still is. They've been together since they were teenagers. They could never have children of their own, though." Cruz's expression changed and the brief glimpse of compassion she'd seen was gone. "That's why Miguel married you, Julia. He wanted a son and he believed you would give him one. Just as you did."

She began to shake uncontrollably, the shock too overwhelming to suppress.

Her throat moved as she swallowed. "You're crazy! I don't believe it! Why would he assume—"

"I can't explain Miguel's thinking." Cruz dropped his hands and took a step backward. In the candlelight, his jaw looked like granite. "All I can tell you is what he did."

"But he could have had anyone. Why me?" Once again she felt as if he knew more than he was letting on. "Why me?" she repeated.

"I can't answer that."

"Can't or won't?"

"The reason he picked you isn't important right now."

"You're right." She capitulated so abruptly she saw his surprise before he could hide it. "The only thing that matters is my son. No one's going to raise that child except me."

"And just how do you plan on doing that if you don't know where he is?"

She took a deep breath and steadied herself. "I'll figure it out."

"And did I mention that time is of the essence?"

"I know that, yes."

"You know that but only because I told you!" For the first time, his impatience revealed itself. "This isn't the only thing out there waiting to trip you up. I can guarantee you there's a shitload of problems you don't know anything about. They're going to jump up and bite you on the ass when you least expect it. You're going to get killed or at the very least, beaten half to death for trying to get away again." His mouth was an angry tight line. "If you have some harebrained scheme to try and leave here on your own again, you won't make it. Are you being stubborn or are you just plain stupid?"

"I'm neither," she said tightly. "But I have too much on the line to trust a total stranger. Why should I believe you can do a better job at getting me out of here than I can do myself?"

JULIA GOT DRESSED after that, Cruz turning his back. She had no idea he could see her reflection in a glass-covered print on the wall and he didn't bother to tell her. She dropped the sheet, reached for her bra and panties, then slipped them on, her movements graceful because her body was so lean. He couldn't make out the particulars, of course, but Cruz had a good imagination and eyes that were accustomed to seeing in the dark. Mentally filling in the shadows with his own details, he felt himself respond. He cursed silently and closed his eyes. When he looked again, she was pulling her silk sweater over her head. He turned around, his thoughts going back to the doubt she'd expressed. Having his abilities questioned was a new experience for Cruz. Most people simply looked at him and decided he knew what he was doing.

"I take it this means you're not going to help me?" He let his eyes drift to her neckline then back up.

"Take it however you like," she said. "All I want is to be left alone." She reached for the silk scarf that was lying on the table, but froze when he grabbed her wrist.

"That's not the answer I wanted to hear," he said.

"I don't care what you want. I only care about my son. I'm getting him back and then the two of us are out of Colombia. Somehow."

He let a minute pass, then he said, "If you can help me, then I can help you."

His words lingered in the tension between them, his offer, if that was what it was, shifting and growing like a living thing. She spoke softly in the silence. "Are you trying to trade me my son's life for my husband's?"

"How could I do that?" he asked. "I don't know where your son is, remember?"

"Right." She drew the word out, her eyes darkening, their color going from a pale shade of azure to something more intense. "I've learned a thing or two since I got to San Isidro. There's one important lesson I've come to understand better than all the others, though. It's the reason I don't want your help."

She spoke in measured tones, but her composure was thin, as if it would tear at any moment.

"And that is?"

"I don't trust you. And I'm not getting involved with anyone I don't trust, especially where my son is concerned."

Cruz let her words soak in, but it was her expression that told the real story. Behind her mask of bravado and relentless determination, there was guilt. Ramirez had destroyed her ability to trust, but she blamed herself as much as she blamed him. Cruz recognized the emotion because he'd seen it in the eyes of Stratton O'Neil. When good people made mistakes, they blamed themselves more than anyone else. He wondered if she knew how pointless her remorse was.

"You probably shouldn't trust me," he began quietly. "I'm not the guy next door and it's been a while since I saw the inside of a church, but that doesn't mean I can't help you."

"That's not why I feel the way I do," she said, surprising him again. "Despite what you say, helping me isn't the main reason you want Miguel dead. It's not even a distant second. You just think that's what I want to hear." She paused. "*My* biggest priority is my son. But, if things go wrong, your agenda will come first. *That's* what bothers me the most."

Once again, he was surprised by her astuteness. "I understand," he said. "But I've been sent here to do a job. That job involves you, yes, but I don't need your permission to complete it. Your help would make it easier, but I've done this for years and I'm still standing. Maybe you ought to think about what that means."

She held herself stiffly, her spine straight. Her expression was equally unyielding. "I don't have to think about it. It means you've killed a lot of people."

"I have," he conceded.

"Here's a newsflash. Killing doesn't impress me. I'm married to Miguel Ramirez. Any coward can kill. What takes real guts is to live when all you really want to do is die."

CRUZ LEFT as silently as he'd come. One minute he was standing in front of her, the next, he was gone. Before he disappeared, though, he made himself clear. He'd be back, and whether Julia trusted him or not, he was going to set his plans into motion.

Julia let herself slump against the massage table, a wash of weakness taking away the front she'd put on for Cruz, as well as the strength from her legs.

She'd thought she had plenty of time but she obviously didn't. Panic, deep and dark, rushed over her as she let herself realize what that meant. No more planning. No more preparation. No more study. She and Tomas had to leave and leave now.

But where *was* Tomas?

For a second, her rage overtook her terror. Damn Miguel to hell! If Cruz was telling the truth, Miguel's plan to take Tomas away from her was the cruelest thing she'd ever heard of and Miguel had already exposed her to a world of pain. Even if her own life depended on it—and it probably did—she couldn't articulate the depth of her reaction to Cruz's news.

Her single comfort came from knowing that Tomas was all right. When Cruz had said he was, strangely enough, she'd believed him more than she had when Miguel had told her the very same thing. Had Miguel taken him out of the country, though? Who exactly *was* Amalia Riveria? And how could Miguel think she could raise Tomas instead of Julia?

Tears gathered in the back of her throat. When she and Miguel had first met, she'd shared the hopes of every woman in love. She'd fantasized about a devoted husband, a fulfilling life, a loving family. Instead, she'd gotten Miguel. How had this happened? How could she have been so blind?

The questions weren't new. Lying in the dark, dreading the sound of his footsteps, she'd asked herself the same things countless times before. But hearing of this latest depravity, she added a new one. What kind of madman *married* a woman for the sole purpose of providing another woman a child? Miguel thought of himself as a devout Catholic. In his twisted mind, did a marriage somehow negate his sins of rape and lying? And why her? Cruz had stepped over that question as if it were a land mine. Did he know the answer or did he simply not care?

Julia pondered the idea for a moment more, then she straightened and walked toward the sink in the back of the room. Turning on the tap, she stuck her hands beneath the stream of cold water and splashed her face to erase the redness her tears had left behind. What she really wanted to do was cleanse herself from the filth Miguel had brought into her life, but she couldn't wash it down the drain no matter how hard she scrubbed. A few minutes later, she headed down the hallway with renewed determination.

Portia was already waiting at their usual table beside the pool. She looked up as Julia approached and Julia saw instantly that the older woman looked refreshed. Her eyes no longer looked tired and her skin had regained its glow. She'd simply been tired and her massage had served her well. She smiled as Julia neared and pulled out a chair.

"I already ordered salads for both of us," she said. "I hope that's all right. I'm starving for some reason."

"That's fine," Julia replied. "But you should have gotten something more substantial. I think you've lost some weight."

Waving her hand, Portia pooh-poohed the remark.

"I'm getting old, that's all. Don't you know old people shrink?"

"You're not *that* old."

"Oh, yes, I am," she replied. "But let's leave it at that, shall we?" She shot a quick glance around the al fresco dining area then leaned closer to Julia. "Have you seen him?"

Julia opened her mouth, but "no" came out instead of the truth. While Portia knew a lot about what went on between Julia and Miguel, she didn't know it all. Some of the more intimate details were just too embarrassing to share, but more than that, a deep sense of self-preservation kept Julia from telling her everything. She loved the older woman…but as she'd told Cruz, she didn't trust anyone completely.

She patted Julia's hand. "Don't worry," she said. "I'm sure he meant what he said. He's going to help you. He has to."

Julia looked at her with a frown. "What do you mean, he *has* to?"

"If your friend sent him here to get you out, then he's obligated," she said with a frown. "That's all I meant."

Portia's explanation sounded sensible, but a growing nervousness began to trouble Julia. Something wasn't right.

The waiter brought their salads, refilled their water glasses, then left them alone. No one liked to be seen hovering near Julia. They were likely to lose their jobs—or their lives—if they appeared more interested in her than what their service required.

Portia began to eat while Julia picked at her salad. Spearing her second tomato slice, Portia glanced at Julia, her fork in midair. Studying Julia's face, she put down her utensil. "I'm sure Miguel would do nothing to harm Tomas, Julia. He dotes on the boy. You realize that, don't you?"

As Portia spoke, Julia's thoughts began to coalesce and all at once she realized what was troubling her. She reached for her water glass to give herself some time to think a bit more. Unless Cruz had lied to her about Miguel's mistress, Julia couldn't imagine why Portia never mentioned the woman.

"I'm sure you're right." Julia put the goblet back down, setting it precisely on the circle it'd left on the tablecloth. "But he should have told me where he was taking him. Every mother needs to know where her child is."

Picking up her fork once again, Portia nodded. "You're right, of course, and as you well know, I'm certainly not one to defend Miguel. But I really don't think he'd hurt his own son."

"I don't think he would, either," Julia said. "But he had to have gotten someone to stay with Tomas last night when he came to confront me about the matches. He was very angry."

"What did you tell him?"

Julia recounted the lie she'd told her husband.

"And he accepted that?"

"From what Guillermo said on the way over, I'd say he did, but who knows? Miguel is very good at keeping secrets."

"He has to be," Portia replied. "His business depends on it."

"As does his personal life." Waiting for her friend to look at her, Julia said no more. Portia didn't respond. She kept her eyes on her salad, a slice of avocado capturing her full attention.

Julia leaned closer. "Miguel has one important secret that I didn't know about until just recently. Do you know what that secret is, Portia?"

Her knuckles tightened on her fork and knife. "If it's a secret, how would I know it?"

"It's one of those things that everyone pretends they don't know but they do. You're very well connected in San Isidro. I think you do know, but for some reason you've kept it from me."

Portia lifted her gaze. "I don't know what you're talking ab—"

Julia didn't let her finish. "I just found out Miguel has a mistress named Amalia Riveria. They've been together for years, even before I arrived here as his wife."

"I didn't—"

Julia shook her head. "You know everything that happens in San Isidro so you knew this. You *had* to." She paused. "Why didn't you tell me about her?"

CHAPTER SIX

PORTIA LET her fork slide from her fingers then reached for her glass of water. Julia waited. Finally, the older woman managed to compose herself and speak.

"I didn't want to tell you about Amalia because you have enough pain in your life." Her low voice was quiet and sincere. "I thought it best you didn't know."

She raised her eyes and Julia read the truth there. Portia knew the woman was Miguel's mistress, but she didn't have a clue about the rest of it. Was Cruz's story just that…a story?

"Who is she?" Julia asked.

"A local girl. Her father worked for Miguel's father and the two grew up together. They were inseparable."

"Why didn't he marry her?"

Portia shrugged her fragile shoulders in a way that explained everything. "I have no idea, Julia. She was poor and uneducated. Maybe he wanted a woman he considered to be his equal…"

Julia kept her expression neutral as Portia's explanation drifted into silence. When she spoke, she made her voice equally disinterested. "Where does she live?"

"No one knows," Portia answered. "Rumor has it that Miguel built her a villa in the mountains years ago, but that's just gossip. I don't know for sure."

"In the mountains? You mean toward Sierra Madrone?"

Portia shook her head at the name of the village. Nestled in the north, it was the only one of any size between San Isidro and Cali. "Farther away than that, I think."

"Do you know her?"

"Yes." Portia took another sip of water. "I know her."

Julia waited for Portia to say more, but the older woman remained silent. After a full minute had passed, maybe even more, Julia prodded her. "Portia?"

"Why do you want to know the details, darling? They mean nothing to you."

"Mark it up to curiosity," Julia replied. "I think any woman in my place would want to know."

"Perhaps, but you aren't just any woman. And Miguel isn't just any husband."

"Maybe that's exactly why I need to know." Julia held Portia's gaze until the elderly woman looked away. "Tell me about her, Portia. Tell me everything. I have to know."

Portia took her time answering, but when she did, Julia almost wished she hadn't been so persistent.

"There's a film star, I believe her name is Catherine Zeta something?"

"Catherine Zeta-Jones?"

Portia nodded. "She's very beautiful."

"Yes, she is."

"Well, Amalia shares her look—the dark hair and eyes, the lush body—but in a beauty contest, the movie star would be a distant runner-up to Amalia. Simply put, she is gorgeous."

Had Julia still cared for Miguel, the news might have hurt. But her only concern was Tomas.

"Do they have children?" Julia wondered if Portia's answer would match Cruz's.

Portia shook her head. "No. They have no children. She's his mistress, Julia. Mistresses are not kept to bear children. That's what wives are for."

Mistaking Julia's anxiety for her son as something else, Portia reached across the table and took Julia's cold fingers in her own. "Amalia represents a separate part of Miguel's life, Julia. Americans don't understand, but this is the Latin way. It's not unusual."

"I couldn't care less that he has a mistress. He could have dozens and it wouldn't matter to me. You should know that by now. Frankly, I'm more bothered by the fact you didn't tell me about her."

"You already had so much to worry about." She

dabbed at her mouth with her napkin, then looked up, her expression contrite. "Please don't be upset with me, Julia. Amalia Riveria isn't important enough to damage our friendship."

"I agree completely." Julia patted her friend's hand. "Like you said, she doesn't matter, one way or the other."

They chatted for another twenty minutes, then walked to the lobby together. Seeing Guillermo, Portia hugged Julia tightly.

"Take care of yourself," she whispered. "And let me know if you hear from Mr. Cruz." She pulled back slightly and looked into Julia's eyes. "I have a good feeling about him. You should trust him. I think he'll help you."

"I hope so." Julia returned Portia's embrace then watched as she crossed the lobby. At the threshold, she turned and waved then passed through the door. The sunshine outside the hotel's overhang was so strong Portia vanished as she stepped into its brightness.

Portia's reason for not telling Julia of Amalia's existence sounded reasonable. She and Julia had a very close relationship, almost mother-daughter, and Julia could see her not wanting to bring any more sadness into Julia's life. Still, the idea of Portia keeping the matter to herself troubled Julia.

Her eyes narrowed in thought, she stared into the blinding light. Everyone had secrets in San Isidro, even, it seemed now, her very best friend.

LATER THAT EVENING and a mile south of the Intercontinental Hotel, where he'd confronted Julia, Cruz stood in the shadow of a run-down warehouse and watched the doorway of the bar across the street.

Fifteen minutes earlier, he'd seen the man he was supposed to meet enter the dive. Any moment now, he was going to come back out with a scowl on his face, angry at being stood up. When he got halfway back to his car, a beat-up Land Rover he'd parked two streets over, Cruz would confront him. At that point, when Cruz knew they were alone, they'd have the conversation the cop had expected to have inside the *cantina*.

In the meantime, Cruz let his thoughts return to Julia Vandamme. Her anger at his revelations hadn't been a surprise, of course, but the way she'd handled herself had been. She didn't rant or rave or even cry. Her only reaction had been a slow stoking of the fire that burned deep inside her. She thought Cruz didn't know how hot that flame of hatred was, but he was beginning to. Her very lack of emotion gave away the secret better than any words could have.

Still, if she didn't make her decision shortly, he would have to do something to goad her into making one. He had plenty of bad news he could use, but the heat any of it would generate could just as easily flare up at him. Julia was exactly the kind of woman he'd fallen for before and, seeing her reflection in the massage room, Cruz had easily imagined the smoothness of her skin and the fragrance in her hair. The realization jarred him. He didn't need a refresher course on how painfully those relationships could end.

Across the way, the door of the bar burst open.

The man who staggered out was the same one Cruz had arranged to meet, Raul Jimenez. Indignation underlined his drunken expression—he'd been stood up and he wasn't happy. In San Isidro, the tiny police force was on Ramirez's payroll, not the city's. The half-dozen men were figures to be feared more than respected, and anyone who made them unhappy paid for their mistake. Two seconds passed, then three more men came out of the bar. Just as Cruz had expected, Jimenez had brought his friends. Cruz caught only snatches of their muted conversation, but he didn't need to hear more. A flash at the waist of one of them caught the neon light above the doorway. They'd been armed. Had it been a setup from the beginning or did they merely want more money?

Their discussion ended. Jimenez hitched up his pants, looked down the street, then started walking. The others went in the opposite direction.

Cruz fell in behind the cop, his steps silent, his breathing measured. It wouldn't surprise him if the other three were doubling back. He'd have to work quickly.

Cruz let Jimenez round the first corner, then waited for him to reach the middle of the block where the shadows went deeper. Timing his steps, he closed the distance between them just as they both entered the darkness.

Cruz slipped in behind the cop, then encircled his neck and bent it to one side. Death was one quick movement away. "Speak and you die." For good measure, Cruz tightened his grip. *"¿Comprendez?"*

The man tried to gasp but gagged instead. He nodded his answer and, backing into the doorway of a small *tienda,* Cruz pulled the cop with him, their awkward dance a blur to anyone who might be looking.

"I saw your friends," Cruz whispered. "You didn't tell me you were planning a party."

Jimenez's voice was hoarse and it smelled like beer. "They were in the bar when I got there. I didn't plan any—"

Cruz jerked his arm, cutting off the empty explanation. "Forget it. We had a deal and you just tried to screw me."

"No, no!" The cop put his hands on Cruz's arm, but they both knew he didn't have a chance in hell of prying Cruz's grip from his throat. "I wasn't trying to do anything like that, *señor.* I had no idea they were going to be there."

"Do you have the information you promised me?"

He nodded frantically then made the mistake of reaching behind him. Thinking the cop was going for his gun, Cruz released the man's neck and grabbed his arm instead, yanking it sideways then upward, pushing down at the same time. Jimenez's shoulder joint snapped out of its socket with an audible click, but his horrified scream ended before it could even start as Cruz pulled on his arm a second time.

"No gun..." Jimenez gasped out. "No gun. It's the *plano*. It...it's in my pocket. Oh, God..."

His legs went out from beneath him and he sagged against Cruz's chest. Thrusting his hand into the man's pocket, Cruz found a piece of folded paper, then stepped back and let him drop to the pavement. Jimenez moaned as Cruz studied the crudely drawn house plan.

After a second, Cruz knelt, the scrap clutched in his hand. "Are you sure this is right?"

Jimenez didn't reply and Cruz slapped him. "Is this accurate?" he asked again.

"*Sí, sí, señor.* It's correct, I swear. My cousin works at the *señorita's* house. She drew it for me."

"If she works there, why can't you tell me where the damn thing's located?"

"They blind her, *señor.* The car comes, it picks her up, they drop her off. She cleans the house, then she goes home, her eyes covered again."

"How long is the drive? How fast do they go? Is it bumpy or smooth? Are they heading west in the evening or—"

The man shook his head then groaned at the movement. "The road is paved part of the way and then it goes rough. From her house in the village, she said she thinks it takes about half an hour. She has no idea about the direction. It could be ten, fifteen, maybe twenty klicks. That's all she knew."

"And the boy is there now?"

The cop leaned over and spit, his lip somehow bloodied by their tussle. "Yes, but if they find out she told me that, they'll kill her twice—once for the *chico* and once for the plans."

Cruz managed to get a few more details from the man, then he folded the piece of paper and crammed it in his pocket. "This info better be good, Jimenez. If I discover it isn't, you're going to regret it."

"I promise—"

"Do you know Jorge Guillermo?"

At the name of Ramirez's bodyguard, the cop's eyes fluttered wildly. "Everyone knows Señor Guillermo. I know him, yes."

"Well, so do I. Obviously we're not friends, but as you can tell, I'm a very convincing fellow. If this information is bad, Señor Guillermo will mysteriously find out that you gave it to someone in return for a very large sum of money. You know what would happen next, don't you?"

Cradling his arm, the cop nodded numbly.

Cruz stood and looked down at the cop. "I'm disappointed with you, Jimenez. Anyone with half a brain would have met me alone, but you tried to bring your buddies in on the deal. That was a big mistake." He stared into the dark street then focused again on the man lying at his boots. "I'm going to give you some free advice. Don't try to double-cross me. If anyone is waiting for me at Riveria's *casa* I'll come back to San Isidro, and at that point, Señor Guillermo will become the least of your worries."

LATE THAT EVENING Julia sat on the patio just off her bedroom and stared up at the night sky. After she'd moved to San Isidro, she'd found comfort in the realization that her mother, back home in Mississippi, could be doing that, too. She'd fancied herself an amateur astronomer and had often taken Julia into the backyard on hot summer nights to lie in the grass and point out the various constellations. The thought brought a longing for her mother and father and all things familiar. She shook her head. Those days would never come again. If she needed reminding of that she only had to look for the stars her mother had once shown her. Since she was in the Southern hemisphere and the seasons were reversed, nothing looked the same.

If she were a philosopher, she might see the parallel. Everything in her life, even the sky, had been turned upside down since she'd met Miguel.

Turning her attention to the table by her chair, she looked at the photograph she'd carried outside. Tomas was a mirror image of his father, except for his personality, thank God. He'd been a sweet and loving child from the day they'd come home from the hospital. She couldn't imagine living without him. Only a few days had passed since Miguel had taken him on their trip and the ache from his absence was unbearable. How would she feel if she never saw her son again? The bombshell that Cruz had dropped was all she'd been able to think about since leaving the hotel.

She didn't have to wonder what her mother would think about her grandson and the life Julia was now leading. Julia had had no communication with her parents in months. They had begged her not to make the mistake of marrying Miguel, but she had ignored them and now they wanted nothing to do with her. She didn't blame them.

The low hum of a single-engine airplane caught her attention. Private planes were continually coming and going, even at night, over San Isidro. When she'd first arrived, she'd asked Miguel about them but he'd immediately blown her off. Listening to conversations he didn't know she heard, she'd figured it out eventually—the planes belonged to either drug runners or DEA agents. They played their cat-and-mouse games without ceasing.

The thought took her full circle, back to Jonathan Cruz. Who was he? Why was he there? What *was* the secret she knew he hid? Had Meredith really sent him to help her or was Julia in for some awful surprise?

Her confusion weighed heavily on her. She didn't

trust Cruz any more than she trusted anyone else she knew. Miguel had taken that ability from her just as surely as he had taken her self-confidence, her freedom, even her love of life.

She thought about the blank expression Cruz had worn as he'd spoken to her about Miguel's murder, then her thoughts turned inward. Who was she to judge? She hadn't exactly experienced the average wife's horror at the possibility of her husband's death, had she? What had Cruz thought of *her*?

Rising to her feet with restless energy, she walked toward the fountain in the center of the patio. Miguel had the gardener put gardenias in the water every evening. The fragrance was heavenly but Julia had come to hate it.

She wanted to leave all of it behind as soon as possible, but was Jonathan Cruz the way to freedom? From the very moment she'd looked into his eyes— when he'd grabbed her wrist after the accident— she'd known he was trouble, but she hadn't expected that trouble to be quite so deadly.

Her thoughts went back to Meredith. She might have sent Cruz to get Julia and Tomas out of San Isidro and kill Miguel but he was there, *first and foremost,* to kill Miguel. Why would Meredith have told him to kill Miguel? Did she think there was no other way? Murder was a drastic solution and there was usually only one reason behind it and that reason was money.

Julia had never pressed Meredith about the business she and her father had started but thinking about it, certain facts occurred to her. Meredith traveled constantly, had business connections in abundance and turned up in the strangest places, always with plenty of cash. Her father had been in Intel and she'd worked for the CIA.

. What was her best friend involved in?

Sitting down on the concrete that circled the fountain, Julia stared at the ghostly white flowers, their pale petals reminding her of bleached bones.

Cruz might be a liar and Meredith, too, but one truth existed that Julia couldn't dispute. A million details she didn't even know about could make her fail if she tried to escape with Tomas on her own again, but only one thing had to go right if she let Cruz help her. Whether she trusted him or not, if he stuck to his word and got her and Tomas out, nothing else would matter.

Dropping her hand into the water, she moved her fingers back and forth, distorting her reflection. The water was dark as blood and almost as warm.

Could she actually murder Miguel in return for that help? Just as importantly, what would happen if she *couldn't* kill him and Cruz did? She didn't doubt his prediction for one minute that she'd end up in jail for the crime.

The worst thing would be if she and Tomas somehow managed to escape and Miguel remained alive.

Miguel, and now Cruz, had told her what would happen if she tried again.

Miguel would hunt them down, kill her and bring Tomas back to Colombia.

Wrapping her shawl around her shoulders, Julia stood. She had a lot of thinking to do. And very little time to do it in.

CHAPTER SEVEN

"ARE YOU SURE about this?" Cruz gripped the receiver to the satellite phone. "How reliable are your sources, Meredith?"

"My sources are as reliable as they always are." Her voice held a tension that was equal to Cruz's. "Ramirez has moved everything up. He called his hired guns and told them to get there ASAP, as well as some of the extra muscle he's using from Guatemala. I don't know when everyone's supposed to arrive, but I'm sure they aren't taking time to smell the flowers along the way. Ramirez has them in high gear."

"This isn't good," Cruz said.

"Tell me something I don't know." She paused. "Do you have any idea where the boy is?"

"I'm pretty sure he's at Amalia Riveria's. My source had plenty of motivation to tell me the truth." His frustration deepened as he spoke. "But I still don't know where the damn house is. Not exactly."

"Does Julia know about the woman?"

"She does now. I told her."

"How'd she take it?"

"She doesn't give a damn, Meredith. All she cares about is her kid. She wants him out of here before Ramirez can turn him into a mini drug dealer. If I've got less time than I thought, though, I'm not sure I can make it all happen when I need to. Do you know why Ramirez moved everything up?"

"I can't answer that," she said. "I was hoping you might know."

"I have no idea and asking Julia about it would be pointless. She knows nothing about that part of the business, but it wouldn't matter anyway. She's not really falling into my arms over this, you know."

"I do know. And I have to admit I'm surprised, Cruz. I thought she'd jump at the chance to get some help." Her voice held a note of apology. "I guess I shouldn't have been insistent that you approach her directly."

"Forget about it," Cruz answered. "You would have been right if Julia hadn't changed, but I have a feeling she's not the same person she was when you two first became friends."

"What do you mean?"

Cruz hesitated and instead of speaking, he looked through the windshield of the car he'd rented. He'd driven out to the closest national *parque,* one of many that dotted the area, to use the satellite phone. On another day, in another time, he would have welcomed the view because it was gorgeous. Thick greenery, hanging flowers of every color, a waterfall in the distance—the vista before him looked like a travel poster, but he appreciated none of it as he wondered how to answer Meredith.

"Julia Vandamme is not the woman you described to me," he said slowly. "She's a lot tougher. A hell of a lot tougher."

"How so?"

"You made me think I'd find a Southern belle, but she's not anything close to that, unless it's the steel magnolia kind and even that description doesn't fit. Mentally and physically, she's got her act together. She's gearing up to get the hell out of Dodge."

"She's always been able to put on a good front," Meredith warned. "She did with me at the party the other night, but I saw the bruises and she couldn't deny them. Are you sure she's not—"

"This is for real," Cruz interrupted. "But she doesn't trust me. And she isn't going to help me until that changes."

"Then you have your work cut out for you," Meredith said. "And time is running out."

"Any suggestions?"

"None but the obvious," she said quietly. "Kill Ramirez the minute you can, then take Julia and the kid and get out as fast as you can. San Isidro's about to break wide-open and there's gonna be blood in the streets."

Cruz ended the call, then opened the car door and

stepped outside. Walking into the thick, dense foliage until he could no longer see the road, he buried the phone a few meters from where he'd hidden it weeks before then camouflaged the disturbed ground. Not a single vehicle had passed since he'd turned off the main highway, but in this part of the world, there was no such thing as being too cautious.

Miguel Ramirez knew that and so did Cruz.

They were two different sides of the very same coin.

SHE'D SWORN OFF the sleeping pills—even half of one—since Miguel had surprised her, so the minute her bedroom door opened, Julia came completely awake. Through the fringes of her eyelashes, she stared into the darkness, her mouth desert dry, her pulse going into overdrive.

A man stood in the middle of her bedroom, his body outlined by the dim light coming through the window behind him. As she watched, he started toward the bed.

She had no idea who he was. He moved so stealthily in the dimness he had to either be familiar with her bedroom or he could see without light. As if he could hear the frantic beating of her heart, he suddenly stopped.

It wasn't Miguel, Julia realized immediately. He was taller and thinner. Was it Cruz? She held her breath and tried harder to see. She couldn't tell for sure, but she didn't see how it could be. Security was lighter when Miguel, and especially Tomas, were gone, but the compound was still patrolled.

She pondered her options with lightninglike speed. She had no weapons, no way to call anyone, and no one to ask for help if she'd had a phone, which she didn't. She lay quietly and tried to decide what to do, her tongue sticking to the top of her mouth. She couldn't even scream, if she'd wanted to.

The man continued across the room, each step bringing him closer to the bed. He moved soundlessly and deliberately, confident in his goal.

He drew nearer, and as he did so, she saw for the first time that he held something in his right hand. It was a pillow. A small white pillow.

He gripped the pillow in both hands, his progress never faltering. He was going to smother her.

She tensed and prepared herself to jump. She'd go straight for him, the element of surprise her only tool. If she could hit him directly in the chest, she could knock him off his feet then flee. He wouldn't have time to react.

Then what? A tiny voice asked. Flee where? To whom? What would she do after that?

Julia didn't know but anything was better than what was fast approaching. As if sleeping deeply, she moaned softly and drew her legs up beneath her. The man froze but as soon as she rested again, his foot-steps resumed.

She let him continue until he was almost at the edge of the bed. As he bent closer she saw that he wore a mask.

He was inches away when she sprang.

She hit him square in the middle of his chest. He grunted in surprise and exhaled sharply, his breath escaping in a loud whoosh.

They tumbled to the floor, but he never lost his hold on the pillow. She had just enough time to note the strangeness of that, then he brought it to her face and pushed her nose against it, one hand holding the pillow, the other one pressing against her throat with a bruising strength.

She reacted automatically, flaying her arms against him and sucking in as much air as she could before he could cut her supply off completely.

Big mistake, she realized a second later. Big... mistake.

The fumes of the chemical on the pillow hit her full force. She gagged once then passed out.

HAVING EVEN LESS TIME than he'd thought he had, Cruz decided to take a chance he would never have taken had things been different.

Climbing over the sill of Julia's window, his main concern was being silent. He'd already slipped mick-eys to two different dogs and held his breath when three sets of guards had passed by—he didn't want to give anyone something more to investigate. After sliding down the wall inside her bathroom, he glided to the door and pushed it open half an inch.

He stared through the slit in disbelief.

He'd arrived just in time to see someone trying to smother her.

Ripping his balaclava from the pocket of his cargo pants, he yanked the black wool over his head then burst into the bedroom.

The masked man looked up in frozen shock. Being interrupted was the last thing he'd expected and Cruz had caught him totally unprepared. Without stopping to analyze what that meant, Cruz took advantage of the situation. He launched himself at the man, and they both went down with hard grunts and flying elbows.

The guy was faster and lighter than Cruz had estimated. He ducked Cruz's first punch and scrambled backward but Cruz recovered quickly. He caught his opponent's leg and jerked him back. The man fell with a thud and Cruz landed a solid right on his jaw. The intruder's mask muffled the sound of Cruz's fist connecting but it didn't diminish the results. Before Cruz could follow up with a left, the guy jumped up, grabbed his pillow and ran.

A second later, he was out the door.

Cruz sprang to his feet to follow then he remembered where he was. Two masked men running out of the bedroom belonging to Miguel Ramirez's wife in the middle of the night would attract more attention than either of them wanted. They'd both be dead before they had time to even think about saying their prayers.

Changing direction, Cruz dashed to the window and stared outside. Her suite was in a separate building, detached from the main part of the house, and her door led directly to a smaller courtyard. Cruz saw only darkness.

Muttering a curse, he went back to Julia. Her face was pale but she was coming to. He picked her up and headed for the bathroom. He made it just in time.

The minute her knees touched the marble, she began to throw up.

Cruz directed her head toward the toilet. She fought him for a moment, then gave in weakly and let him guide her. When she finished, she slumped to the floor and groaned. Grabbing a damp washcloth from the edge of the tub behind them, Cruz handed it to her, but instead of using the towel, she let her hand fall limply to her lap.

Cruz retrieved the cloth, lifted her face with a finger beneath her chin, then washed her cheeks with slow strokes. She closed her eyes in obvious gratitude and let him clean her up. When he finished, he tucked her hair behind her ears then rocked back on his heels.

She moaned hoarsely. "Wh-what happened? I remember someone coming into the room..." She stopped to cough, "Then the next thing I knew—" Her words were cut off by a sudden gasp, her eyes rounding with suspicion as she looked up at him.

"It wasn't me," he said quietly. "I was ten seconds too late or, depending on how you look at it, maybe, ten seconds too early. I didn't catch him, but I did stop him."

Her regard remaining wary. She coughed again then winced. Cruz found himself reaching over to brush his knuckles over her reddened skin.

"Who?" Her voice was a painful rasp.

"You tell me," Cruz asked. "I barely got a glance at him before he took off. Who do you think it was?"

"I—I don't know. He had on a mask." She frowned painfully. "Can I have some water?"

Cruz stepped over her to get to the marble vanity. Ramirez had spared no expense when building his lair. Gold faucets, marble counters, beveled mirrors—the bath was a sybarite's dream. Locating a small crystal tumbler, Cruz filled it from the bottle of water that sat on a copper tray.

She took the glass gratefully.

"Go slow," he warned. "He obviously had something on that pillow."

She nodded while sipping then set the glass down on the floor beside her. "It smelled sweet," she said. "I heard him come in and I saw him walking toward the bed. I was waiting for him to get closer but when

I jumped at him, he stuck the damn thing under my nose. It was awful. I tried to fight him, but it was pointless. My whole throat's burning and feels raw." She looked at him. "You saved my life."

"Maybe," Cruz conceded.

She frowned then shook her head, her fingers going back to her throat. "This doesn't feel like 'maybe.'"

"If he'd wanted to kill you, he wouldn't have been trying to knock you out. Why bother? He would have just strangled you and left."

When she gasped at his words, Cruz felt a moment's regret. He'd been out of polite society for too long—he'd forgotten that not everyone addressed the subject of death and killing as bluntly as he did.

"He probably wanted to kidnap you," Cruz said. "You'd be a valuable hostage."

"Miguel's always been terrified of kidnapping," she said faintly. "He's constantly warning me about Tomas, about how I should never take him anywhere without Guillermo." She shook her head. "Whoever they are, they'd would have been in for a rude awakening. Miguel wouldn't bother to pay a ransom for me."

"Maybe so, but who knows how he treats you besides you and me?" Cruz asked.

"Good point," she said. "And Miguel probably would pay despite what he thinks of me."

"Why is that?" Cruz frowned in obvious confusion.

"He wouldn't want anyone thinking they'd gotten the better of him." Her voice was bitter. "He might not want me, but he wouldn't want anyone else having me, either."

Even though she no longer cared, the pain her reasoning caused her was obvious. Cruz felt a flash of sympathy for her. "This isn't the time or the place to analyze the problem," Cruz said to divert her. "I've already stayed too long as it is."

He extended both hands and Julia took them, pulling herself to her feet with a low grunt. She swayed, and Cruz had to put his arm around her waist to steady her.

"Everything's spinning," she said faintly.

"I'm sure it is," he said, "and it probably won't stop for a while. You might want to take it easy for a bit. And don't eat anything for at least two hours. There's a local herb he could have used that's stimulated again by eating."

She stumbled slightly and Cruz tightened his grip, her silk nightgown providing no barrier between them. He could have been touching bare skin, the warmth of her hip searing his fingers and making its way into his brain where he knew the memory would keep him awake. His own body responded, and he cursed himself under his breath, but it did little good.

She misinterpreted his response. "You don't need to help me anymore. I—I can walk."

He ignored her words and led her to the bed,

where she sat down just as her legs went out from beneath her.

"Damn." She put her hand to her head and closed her eyes.

"We have to talk," Cruz said. "But not here. Meet me at two at Portia's."

Julia's eyes opened and she frowned. "I don't—"

"This changes things, Julia." He was there because of Meredith's warning, but the intruder had made things easier for him. He tilted his head to the door at his back. "Someone wants to hurt you and time's running out."

"All I care about is Tomas."

"That's fine. But if you're not here, then you can't very well take care of him, can you?"

Her teeth clicked together as her jaw snapped shut.

"Meet me tomorrow," he ordered. "And for God's sake, don't tell anyone what happened here tonight."

JULIA DIDN'T THINK she'd sleep, but the minute her head hit the pillow, she was out. When she woke up four hours later, she felt as if she were emerging from a weeklong drunk. But she was alive, thanks to Cruz.

She took a long, hot shower and thought hard about what had happened. The fog of whatever drug had been on the pillow was still lingering in her brain, though, and in the end, she gave up trying to make sense of the events. One question seemed to outweigh the others: How in the hell had Cruz—and her attacker—both gotten inside the compound without anyone knowing?

She dressed and called Portia.

"I'd like to come see the new kitchen," she said in a rasping voice when Portia answered. "Your paint job is finished, right? I got those fabric samples I told you about."

"Oh, wonderful!" Portia's tone became excited as she began to understand. Julia had seen Cruz and wanted to tell Portia what he'd said. "When can you come?"

"I was thinking about this afternoon, if that would be convenient?"

"That would be perfect, sweetheart. But you don't sound right. Your voice is hoarse. Is something wrong?"

"I have a sore throat," Julia said lightly. "Nothing too bad. Just my allergies acting up, I think."

They chatted for a bit more, then said their goodbyes, Portia promising to look for Julia after lunch.

Returning to her bedroom with the intention of working on her escape plans, Julia locked her door and pulled out her maps, but once they were spread before her, she found her thoughts returning to the night before just as she'd known they would.

Who had tried to kidnap her? How had they gotten into her bedroom? If Cruz hadn't intervened where would she be right now?

Her questions rattled around like marbles in a glass jar, making lots of noise but with very little purpose. Finally they stopped moving and settled on one subject—Cruz.

She'd felt horrible last night but not so much that she'd failed to realize how gentle he'd been when he'd cleaned her up and helped her back to the bed. That kind of softness was the last thing she would have expected from Cruz. It seemed so contrary to the rest of him that she wondered for a bit if she was embellishing what had really happened. Could his fingers have really felt that warm? Could his touch have really been that sympathetic?

After a bit she decided she was confused. Cruz wasn't a man who cared—he was a man who killed.

So why did this even matter to her? She no longer had the luxury of depending solely on herself. She had to get Tomas out of San Isidro and do so quickly. Like Cruz had said, if she wasn't here, how could she protect her son?

She went back to her maps with renewed determination, but it took her less than an hour to figure out what had pulled at her memory after discussing Miguel's mistress with Portia. She studied the lines and dots for another hour, though, just to confirm her suspicions.

Finally, Julia pushed her chair back and stood up to stretch, her hands on her hips as she twisted and turned. She turned back to the charts one more time

then, after a minute, nodded her head. As she hid
them once again, a small secret smile lifted her lips.

PORTIA GREETED Julia at the door with a kiss on both
cheeks. Cruz watched from the safety of a nearby incline, his binoculars steady, his mind a little less so.
He couldn't stop thinking about what would have
happened if he hadn't been at the villa. If the attack
on Julia had been Miguel's doing, Cruz was going
to have more trouble on his hands than he needed,
but his reaction went even deeper than that. He
fought the feeling instead of acknowledging it.

Julia Vandamme meant nothing to him. She was
a means to an end and when he finished his business
in San Isidro, she'd be out of his life. He would have
money in his pocket for the killing of Miguel Ramirez, and he would be ready for the next job. And
then the next one. And then the next one. Julia, or for
that matter, any woman, had no place in his existence
and Cruz intended to keep things that way.

So dammit, why did he keep thinking about her?

He put the binoculars into the pack beside him,
then started down the rocky slope. Winding his way
through the alleys and unpaved streets, Cruz came
out a few minutes later at Portia Lauer's unlocked
garden gate. He slipped inside.

Standing by Portia's outdoor table, Julia was lost
in thought, no doubt wondering why Portia had left
the house once she'd opened her front door to let

Julia in. She'd left because Cruz had told her to. He'd lied and given her a perfectly logical reason explaining his need for privacy and she'd accepted his words without question. She wasn't capable of thinking about what he might have to do next.

As the gate clicked behind Cruz, Julia raised her head and looked directly at him. She made no sound but she lifted her fingers to the silk scarf she wore at her neck as if he'd been the one who caused the marks it hid.

It always came down to this. Life or death. She knew too much. If she wasn't going to help him, then he had to make sure she didn't help anyone else. Despite the promise he'd made to Meredith, they all knew that killing Miguel Ramirez was Cruz's job. Helping Julia was only an added extra.

He had to either gain Julia's trust or he had get rid of her. He wasn't sure he could do the first, but he was even less confident he could do the second.

CHAPTER EIGHT

JULIA WATCHED Cruz cross the patio. He moved smoothly, his steps silent. She could imagine him slipping over the walls of the compound last night and then into her bedroom without waking a soul. She remembered him helping her into bed and the image shifted unexpectedly from reality to fantasy. Shivering at what she thought of next, she thrust the idea from her mind.

He reached her side. "Where's Portia?" he asked in lieu of a greeting.

Swallowing nervously, Julia answered. "She told me she had to leave. Something unexpected came up."

He nodded as if he had expected her answer then he walked to the loggia next to the house. An arbor-like roof of rough timbers covered with climbing wisteria shaded the outdoor room, creating shadows and more importantly for Cruz, she suspected, privacy. She followed him, leaving the afternoon sun behind.

"Did Guillermo bring you?" he asked.

"No," she said. "I drove myself. Guillermo had to

go out of town. He left the keys and one of the men he trusts, but I bullied him and said I'd get him fired if he came with me. I told him I come here alone all the time and there was little he could do. I had the keys—I just got in the car and left."

"I thought you were more restricted than that."

She ducked her eyes, a flush of embarrassment at her lack of control over her own life warming her cheeks. "There's never more than a gallon of gasoline in the tank and even if I could find someone willing to sell me some fuel, I have no money."

He made no comment, and she sat down before the outdoor fireplace on a sofa with padded cushions. Expecting Cruz to take the chair to her left, Julia watched uneasily as he dropped to the couch beside her.

"I make you nervous." It was a statement of fact, not a question. "Even though I'm here to help you."

"Yes, you do," she admitted. "I think you have more on your mind than merely helping me, and ulterior motives always make me anxious."

"I told you last time my motives aren't an issue." He shifted his weight so that he faced her. His position was a casual one, but there was nothing relaxed about his body or the attention he focused on her. Draping his left arm on the back of the cushions, he reached over and pulled off her scarf, exposing her neck. His fingers grazed the bruised skin where her assailant had held her down. "Does it hurt?"

"I'm sore," she admitted.

"Who did this?" he asked, his voice thoughtful. "Who got past your walls, walked through your compound and made their way into your bedroom without anyone knowing?"

Almost absentmindedly, it seemed to Julia, he rubbed his finger on her neck then leaned back against the cushion and wrapped her scarf around his fist. She suppressed the shiver that threatened. It'd been years—literally—since a man had touched her with anything but harshness and that, combined with her earlier thoughts, were enough to unsettle her.

She spoke sharply in an effort to distract herself. "I would imagine you could answer that better than me—you did the very same thing, didn't you?"

"I did," he answered, "but few others could. Who knows Miguel's gone?"

"Any number of people within his organization but outside that, he tells very few what he's really doing. Why would Miguel want to kidnap me, though? That doesn't make any sense."

Cruz leaned closer and she caught the scent of fresh cedar, the kind that came from the tree, not aftershave. He'd been outside doing something.

"Maybe he didn't want to kidnap you. Maybe he wanted it to look like a kidnapping but later he was going to kill you." He paused and formed his words carefully. "If that is the case, we're in trouble."

"Why is that?"

"He'll know someone rescued you. And that's not a good thing."

Her stomach turned over. "Oh, God, I never thought of that. Wh-what are you going to do?"

"Pray it wasn't him and do what I was going to do anyway. I can't change what happened now."

"He's had plenty of time and plenty of opportunity to kill me before this point. Why now?"

"You've accomplished the goal he had, which was to give him a son. Does he want more children?"

"I don't know, but he won't be having them with me, that's for sure."

Cruz stood and walked to the fireplace, his back to her as he spoke again. "Well, whoever the SOB was, I interrupted his plans. I wouldn't be surprised if he tried again." He turned. "Next time you might not be as prepared or as lucky. I've got to find Miguel before this happens again. Are you sure you don't know where he might be?"

"He told me nothing about his plans. I don't have a clue."

"Does he leave the country often?"

"No, he's afraid to be gone that long."

"So, he's probably still in Colombia?"

"I would guess so."

"Has he got family around here?"

"He never talks about his family. He told me they're all dead but I don't know anything more."

"So his only real connection here—besides you

and Tomas—is the mistress..." Cruz's voice died out as he worked through the problem.

Julia pushed up from the cushions and came to where he stood. She wouldn't get a better opportunity than this very moment.

"I don't know where he is, but..." She paused and swallowed. "I'll help you find him. I—I decided I want to help you do what you came here to do."

Julia read his body language and knew immediately she wasn't imagining Cruz's response. Not only did his brow clear, the tension seeped from his shoulders, and his hands, which had been fisted at his side, relaxed and opened. Her pronouncement had greatly relieved him. Why? What had her answer saved him from?

His voice was noncommittal, despite the effect her decision had had on him. "You made a wise choice."

"My cooperation isn't free, though," she said slowly. "You have to pay for it, Cruz, and if you don't like my terms, you'll like what happens afterward even less."

HE WASN'T ACCUSTOMED to being threatened. "You aren't in a position to bargain," he said.

"Oh, no? Well, I think you're forgetting something." Her eyes blazed with a sudden inner fire. "I *am* the wife of Miguel Ramirez and that still means a lot in San Isidro."

He started to tell her she was wrong. But he silenced himself. This wasn't the time. "What are you saying?"

"I can make you disappear," she said. "All I have to do is tell Miguel who you are. You'd be dead before you even knew he was after you."

Cruz's gut went tight and his patience evaporated. "You could take me down," he agreed, "but you'd be next. How would that help anything?"

"I haven't survived this long without learning a few tricks of my own. Things might not be too pleasant for a while, but I'm a patient woman. Sooner or later, I'd get another chance to leave."

"What about the person who tried to grab you?"

"Miguel is Colombian," she answered. "You don't take what they consider their own without a fight. The value of what you've taken is the least important issue."

"And your son? What would happen to him while you were waiting?"

"I'll figure that out if I need to," she answered. "I can think on my feet."

Cruz looked at her with a steady gaze and she looked right back, her blue eyes as clear and faultless as the sky overhead. He decided she was bluffing. She wasn't the kind of woman who would gamble with something as important as her son.

But she had balls, he'd give her that much.

Playing along, he feigned disgust. "What are these terms?"

"I want my son back first. Once I know he's safe, then…" She paused as if what she wanted to say was difficult. He realized it probably was. "Then I'll help you kill Miguel."

He was shaking his head before she even finished. "That would never work. The minute Tomas went missing, Miguel would go nuts and everything would be crazy. I wouldn't have a chance in hell of hitting him after that. That plan is way too risky—"

She put her hand on his arm. "You haven't been listening."

He stared down at her.

"I told you earlier Miguel's got a thing about Tomas being kidnapped. If we can find him and grab him, the idea would never enter Miguel's mind that I might have our son. He doesn't see me as capable of doing anything, much less snatching Tomas and hiding him. He'd suspect one of his rivals and he'll rush back—from wherever he is right now—and set up a command post. Instead of having to track him down, you'll know exactly where Miguel is." She gripped his arm harder. "It makes perfect sense, Cruz. We can hide Tomas, I'll play the hysterical mother and you can do whatever you have to do."

"And where do we put Tomas in the meantime?"

"Portia will hide him for us."

There were holes, but her plan did give Cruz some things he hadn't had before—he *would* have Ramirez in one place, but more importantly the man would be preoccupied with his son's disappearance. That meant he'd be distracted, and distraction led to mistakes.

Once again, Julia had surprised him, but Cruz acted unimpressed. "You've got it all figured out, don't you?"

She dropped her fingers from his arm. "Of course, I don't. I'm sure I've forgotten some detail that could blow the whole thing wide-open, but I've done the best I know how. There is one last thing, though."

He raised an eyebrow and looked at her.

She took a deep breath and let it out slowly, her eyes never leaving his face. "After we figure out where Tomas is, you aren't going to get him alone. I have to come with you or the whole deal is off."

"Now I KNOW you're crazy," he said bluntly. "There's no way I'd take you with me. It's too dangerous. You'd get all us killed."

"You have to take me."

"I don't think so."

"I think I know where he is," she said softly.

Cruz looked at her, his empty eyes reminding her of two dark lakes. "I know where he is, no thinking about it. Your son is at the home of Amalia Riveria. Miguel took him there. My sources confirmed that."

She studied him. "Are you sure he's there? And he's okay?"

"He was as of the night when I got the info."

She nodded, something that felt like joy washing over her. "Do you know where Amalia lives?"

"No." He shook his head slowly. "Do you?"

"I do and if you don't take me, I'll go on my own."

Before Julia could even sense any movement, Cruz had her trapped, her illusion of power flying away as swiftly as Portia's canaries would if someone opened their cage door. He held her still, his hands gripping her shoulders, his thumbs resting at the base of her throat. His hold was tight, but something told her it could get a lot tighter and much more deadly.

"How is it you have this information?" he asked suspiciously. "I only told you about her a few days ago."

"When I confronted Portia about Amalia, I remembered something Miguel said once about an area north of here that he's always loved. I looked at some maps and it all came together. Amalia's house has to be there."

He absorbed what she said, before speaking. "If you try to retrieve Tomas by yourself, you'll die and so will he."

"You're not worried about that," she replied calmly. "All you care about is whether or not I'll be here to help you with Miguel."

The pressure against her throat increased gently. His voice deepened. "I could *stop* you from doing this, Julia."

She swallowed. "I know that," she said, "but you won't."

"I wouldn't put money on that if I were you."

"I'm betting with something more important than money," she countered.

"You'll screw things up."

"No," she said. "*You* will. Because Tomas won't understand. He might not leave with a stranger. He could scream and kick and set up such a fuss everyone in the compound could be alerted. You'd die and he might, too."

His grip eased but he didn't step back. "Are you lying to me?"

"Why would I do that?" she asked. "I want my son back. You're the best chance I have of getting him."

"You didn't think that the other day. You wanted to do this all on your own."

"And I still wish I could," she said. "But I'm not stupid. Even though I don't trust you, last night made me realize I have a better chance of getting away with you helping me." She lifted her hands and put them on his chest. Beneath her trembling fingers, she felt nothing but muscle. There was no warmth, no heartbeat, no breath. Nothing but a rock-solid hardness. "I need you, Cruz. But you need me, too."

Cruz held her tightly, his eyes searching her face as if he could read her mind. He'd accused her of being crazy and, for one long second, she thought he might be right—the only thing she could think about was closing her eyes, pulling him to her and kissing him. Her unexpected desire was so improbable but at the same time, so powerful, she swayed. He steadied her, then released her and stepped back. His nearness had made her shake but his sudden distance left Julia feeling even more strange. What was happening to her?

"What about your absence? If Tomas goes missing, the first thing Miguel will do is look for you."

"Sometimes Portia and I go shopping in Medellin. On occasion we spend the night. As long as I'm not gone too long, Miguel won't care. He has my passport so I can't get too far and he knows it. Portia will cover for me."

Cruz increased the space between them. For one impossible second, she wondered if her nearness affected him as his did her, but she discarded the idea. Cruz was not the kind of man who ever lacked for women and something told her she wasn't the kind he would consider anyway. He wouldn't give a second glance to a woman who'd made the foolish mistakes she had.

He stood for a long time with his back to her, staring out the window that was set in the garden wall, his fingers gripping the iron bars that covered it.

"All right," he said, turning around. "You win. We'll do this your way, but when the time comes you're going to owe me. Do you understand what I'm saying?"

She looked him straight in the eye and nodded. "I understand," she said. "I understand completely."

JULIA PROMISED to meet Cruz the next day and work out the details. She would be taking a risk leaving the compound again so soon but, with Guillermo gone, her absences might go unnoticed. She hoped so, anyway.

As they walked toward the garden gate, Cruz's instructions came as fast as his questions had a few minutes before.

"Be prepared to leave immediately," he was saying. "I won't be able to give you much notice and needless to say, don't tell anyone—including Portia—what we're doing. We'll tell her what we have to when we have to."

They reached the iron gate a few moments later. She hadn't told Cruz about Portia's strange behavior at the hotel the other day because Julia had come to wonder if it *had* been strange. At the time, the older woman had seemed nervous and out of sorts, but, thinking back on it, Julia was unsure of her assessment. Since Cruz had crashed his way into her life, she'd become unsure of a lot of things.

He stopped, his hand on the latch. "I gave you my word," he said quietly, "but I have to ask—are you sure you want to come with me?"

She started to answer, but he raised his hand and put a finger across her lips. "Don't answer me until you hear the rest."

She nodded and he dropped his hand.

"Operations like this don't always go smoothly.

We could run into all kinds of problems. Can you handle that?"

"I guess it depends on the problem," she answered honestly.

"What if we found something unpleasant?"

She should have been prepared when she saw his eyes darken, but she wasn't.

"What if your son isn't there?" he asked. "What if we find him but he's dead?"

His words cut off her breath and it took a second for her to make her lungs work again.

"It's a possibility you need to think about," he warned.

She shook her head numbly. "What purpose would that serve?"

"Absolutely none," he answered, "but when has that ever stopped Miguel from doing anything? He doesn't think like the rest of us, Julia. That's what I'm trying to tell you. You can't fall apart on me, no matter what. You'll get us killed."

"That won't happen," she said resolutely.

Apparently satisfied, he started out the gate, but at the last minute he looked over his shoulder, his eyes dropping to her throat then back to her face. "Watch your back," he said softly. "There are a lot of bad guys out there."

Julia returned to the patio table on shaky legs, Cruz's parting shot haunting her. She'd never thought Miguel would hurt Tomas. Miguel was a Colombian and that meant he valued family. But that also meant he knew the value of her son. He'd never been shy about using Tomas to make Julia cooperate. At the same time, Miguel was well aware of the fact that Julia would never give up her son—if Miguel wanted total control of Tomas there was only one way he was going to get it and that was over her dead body.

CRUZ POWERED UP his laptop and logged on. He had an encrypted machine, but he communicated with Meredith through a code regardless. Posing as teenagers, they met in a chat room and started the conversation by dissing their parents for their most recent lame acts. The conversation became serious when Meredith told him Ramirez had hit one of his minor rivals. The man he'd killed was unimportant to Cruz—none of the undercover people had been part of his setup—but the move confirmed Miguel was eager to start his housecleaning.

Cruz absorbed the news then moved on, telling Meredith the plan. He finished by telling her his "friend" wanted to go with him on "spring break."

You can't let her go, Meredith wrote. She could mess up everything.

I know, Cruz typed. But don't worry. It's not going to happen.

What are you going to do?

He explained what he'd come up with between Portia's house and the hotel. His idea probably wasn't the most well thought out, but given the time he had, it wasn't bad. It might even work. Maybe.

If I don't let her think she's coming, she's threatened to go on her own.

A major disaster.

No kidding.

But what if she's telling you the truth? What if you can't get the package without her?

I'll get it, he answered grimly. One way or another.

They discussed more details, then Cruz ended the conversation by telling Meredith of the kidnapping attempt.

God, is she okay?

She was a little bruised and a little loopy, he replied. But she's fine.

You picked the right time to go in.

I know. The keys rattled beneath his fingers. Which makes me wonder even more. The timing was a little too good.

You think it was planned? Interesting. Why?

Who knows? he asked. This is a crazy place and I'm dealing with some crazier people. Nothing I've seen makes any sense. For all I know it was a trap designed by our guy to see if P is my aunt. If it was, we're screwed.

They would have checked you out before.

You never know for sure.

They logged off after that, Cruz pushing away from the desk. He wasn't lying—nothing *had* made sense to him following his arrival in San Isidro, but that included some of his reactions, especially those involving Julia. Each time he saw her, his awareness of her seemed to sharpen. Last night's encounter had left his senses razor sharp but, unbelievably, this afternoon's session at Portia's had affected him even more.

He couldn't rid himself of the impressions Julia had left behind. Her perfume lingered on his knuckles and the feel of her skin was all he could imagine beneath his fingertips. The fear he'd seen in her eyes haunted him, but so did the way she'd tried to force him into taking her with him. He'd never known a woman so determined yet so vulnerable. She puzzled and intrigued him.

He stood so abruptly, the chair he'd been sitting in rocked back and almost fell. He caught the arm at the very last moment. Still, the legs wobbled a few seconds before they settled. Resting his hands on the chair back, Cruz shook his head and cursed.

He needed to steady his thinking or he was going to go down, too. Nothing reinforced that like his relief when Julia had told him she'd help. Her acquiescence had felt like a reprieve, his own and not hers, and he'd been shocked at the way he'd felt.

Relief and regret weren't part of his vocabulary and he'd be well-advised to remember that.

EVERY FRIDAY, Julia volunteered at the local hospital. She liked to visit with the patients, especially the children, but more often than not she spent her time in the administrator's office writing letters to American charities begging for money and supplies. Miguel could have funded a large portion, *if not all,* of what the place needed. She'd asked him once for help but he'd up and walked away. He simply didn't care if the people of San Isidro suffered. They meant nothing to him. In his eyes, they were worker ants and nothing more.

She finished the letter she'd been writing and

stood to stretch, glancing at her watch. It was almost noon, she saw in surprise, and she was hungry. Catching a glimpse of the cloudless sky, she decided to take the salad she'd brought with her and go to the garden. She didn't have the choice of going out. She'd been dropped off this morning, as always, at the hospital's door by Guillermo, who had returned and resumed his watchdog duties.

As she normally did before lunch, she headed down the corridor to the closet-size restroom to wash up. The hospital was typical for South American institutions and every inch of space was utilized twice. The tiny room she stepped into was no exception. It served as a washroom *and* as the janitor's supply room. After locking the door behind her, she walked to the lavatory and turned on the water.

A heartbeat later, the closet door opened up. She drew in a sharp breath and jerked her eyes to the mirror.

Cruz met her startled gaze.

"We're going tomorrow night," he announced. "How long will it take us to get to Riveria's?"

Julia's wet hand flew to her throat, but she managed to swallow her gasp. "Cruz! My God, you scared me half to death! How in the heck did you—"

"How long will it take?" he repeated, then took a single step in her direction. What little space there had been in the room disappeared as Cruz's long body pressed against her spine.

She blinked and tried to focus. "We can drive part of the way, but we'll have to hike in at the end. Four hours? Maybe five? I don't know exactly."

"You'll have to contact Portia and make the arrangements for your 'shopping trip.' Will she be suspicious? Last-minute trips don't sound like your kind of thing." He lifted his hand to indicate the room where they stood. "You're a very predictable woman, Julia. I could set my watch by your actions."

Stunned by his appearance and even more so by his closeness, Julia had to search for an answer to his observation. "I'm not impulsive, but I don't think Portia will be concerned. I've been anxious lately and she understands why."

"Do you fly or drive?"

"Either."

"This time you're flying," he said. "Make your reservations for a Saturday flight, but make it a different one from Portia's. Have Guillermo drop you off at the airport. I'll find you."

She nodded tensely.

"How long can you be gone?"

"No more than two nights," she said quickly. "That's the rule."

As soon as she spoke, Julia winced, hearing how that must have sounded to Cruz. How pathetic. Rules were for naughty children and rebellious teenagers, not women her age. She could only imagine what he must think of her.

She looked at his face but his expression had shifted. If he *did* think she was a nut, he didn't show it. His eyes went to her neck and he pulled back her collar to examine her throat, just as he had before.

As a breeze rippled in through the window open behind them, Julia thought he might touch her again. He dropped his hands to his side and disappointment washed over her.

"How do you feel?" he asked.

"The soreness is gone—"

He shook his head. "I mean about us leaving. Once we do this thing, there's no going back."

"I understand that. I'm ready."

"You think you can handle everything?"

"I know I can."

He seemed to consider her answer, then apparently satisfied, he moved to the door. Was it her imagination or did he pause for a single heartbeat before squeezing past? She couldn't tell but, either way, the damage was already done. The impression his body left stayed with her for the rest of the day.

CHAPTER NINE

WHEN JULIA CALLED Portia and asked if she'd like to go to Medellin, the older woman immediately accepted the offer, along with Julia's excuse for taking a separate flight later than her own. Any reason to leave San Isidro was a good one and few questions were ever asked, especially if the getaway included Medellin. It was a beautiful city and everyone in Colombia loved it. Cosmopolitan but quintessentially Colombian, its reputation as being a dangerous place was well deserved, but it was also known as *una ciudad con cuerpo*—a city with a body. The nickname came because a local artist, Fernando Botero, had filled the parks and even its metro line stations, with his lush sculptures of corpulent figures, but the tag was appropriate for another reason. Everything in the city, including the peaks of the Cordillera Central that hovered over the valley, touched the senses like a robust red wine.

The two women talked briefly about what they might do, agreeing to meet Saturday evening for dinner at their favorite restaurant.

"I'm so glad you suggested this," Portia said. "I'd actually been thinking about doing it myself. I may just give Chita a few days off and stay even longer. I want to get my hair cut and handle some other errands, too."

Julia closed her eyes in relief. "I think that would be very nice of you. She works hard. Since you aren't going to be there, why not?"

They hung up then and the day passed with excruciating slowness. Julia spent most of the time worrying. What if something went wrong? What if Amalia's house was not where Julia had decided it was? What if Tomas wasn't there? What if, what if, what if… Everything except the possibility of success came into her mind, each scenario progressively worse.

When darkness finally came, she went to bed, but her anxiety wouldn't let her sleep more than a few hours. Unfortunately, those hours came right before dawn. When her alarm sounded, she hit the off button and went back to sleep. The interval that followed felt more like a drug-induced lull than a time for rest and after another couple of hours, she gave up and got dressed. Cruz had been insistent she book the latest flight she could, and the rest of the day went by even slower than the previous one had. By nine that night, when Guillermo finally brought the car around, she'd begun to understand the term "coming unglued." The edges holding her together were slowly dissolving under the onslaught of this incredible stress. If she'd had to wait another hour, she wasn't sure she would have made it.

Guillermo glanced at her as they pulled away from the villa. "When will you be back?" he asked. "I don't want to be late picking you up."

His tone was casual. Julia calmed herself and answered. "I'm returning Monday, sometime before noon. But don't worry. I'll get a cab. You don't need to come back."

He accepted her answer, but his next question made her even more queasy. "Everything go okay while I was gone? You didn't have any problems, did you?"

As far as she knew, no one was aware of the incident in her bedroom except Cruz and the man who'd tried to strangle her. She told herself Guillermo's query was nothing extraordinary—didn't he always ask that same thing when he'd been gone?—but her gut tightened regardless.

She looked out the window. "Everything was fine. Boringly fine."

He answered with a grunt and nothing more was said. As the SUV sped toward the airport, though, Julia's suspicions grew. By the time Guillermo pulled under the canopy at the terminal and stepped around to the back of the vehicle to retrieve her bag, she was sweating.

Guillermo could have been the man behind the mask.

He was tall enough, strong enough, and he definitely knew his way around the compound.

More importantly, no one would have raised an alarm seeing him. He belonged inside the walls, and anything he did there was either approved of by Miguel or done on his direct orders.

She didn't wait for Guillermo to open her door. She stepped out of the SUV and onto the sidewalk in front of the terminal, the vapor lights bathing her in an acid yellow mist.

"I'll take it from here." She reached for the bag in his hand. "You don't have to wait with me. I'm sure you have more important things to do than babysit me."

Their eyes met over the suitcase, each holding onto the handle.

"Not really," he said.

She made her expression frosty. "Well, *I* have better things to do than to give you something to watch. I'm not a child. I can get myself on an airplane." Gripping the case, she pulled it from him and stalked away.

Once inside the terminal, she paused in the shadow of the doors, her heart hammering. Guillermo stood on the sidewalk as if thinking about what to do, then he turned and went back to the SUV. Blocking the traffic behind him, he calmly ignored the feeble protestations of a nearby airport guard and punched out a number on his cell phone.

Was he calling Miguel?

Forcing herself to walk slowly, Julia turned away from the door and proceeded to the checkout counter. With ticket in hand, she made her way past San Isidro's version of security—a guard who waved at her as she passed by—and headed to the boarding area. The airport was tiny, with only three gates, and as she took her seat and prepared to wait, Julia forced herself to put aside her concerns over Guillermo's actions, past and present. If he was going to come inside and stop her from leaving, she'd know about it in a few minutes. Until that happened, she'd wait. She'd learned to do that since marrying Miguel and the coping technique had served her well.

Once she was out of Guillermo's sight, she walked to the nearest pay phone, called the hotel where she and Portia always stayed, and had them ring her room. She was just about to hang up when Portia answered.

"Portia! I'm so glad I caught you." She tried to make her voice sound nervous, which wasn't a stretch at all. "I've got a problem. Miguel called and said he might come home early. If he returns, I want to be here to see Tomas."

"Say no more, Julia. I understand completely."

Julia felt a twinge of guilt at lying to her friend but she continued the charade. Thank goodness, Portia understood Miguel's demands. "I knew you would," she said with feigned relief. "You'll stay, though, won't you? Don't come back on my account."

"I've already made an appointment on Saturday to get my hair done," she said. "I'll be fine, don't worry about me. But will you be okay?"

"As long as I keep him happy, I will be," Julia answered. "You know how Miguel can be, Portia. He may change his mind and stay right where he is. If that happens..." Julia made her voice hesitant "...if that happens and I end up with nothing to do, would you mind terribly if I escaped to your place for a day or two? I'm going to go crazy if I don't get out of here and if I can't be with you, I'd at least like to leave the house for a bit."

"Oh, darling, I wouldn't mind at all. I'd be delighted for you to do just that. My home is all yours."

"Thank you. It's a relief knowing I can do that. I don't think I'll tell Miguel. If he doesn't return and he should call the hotel, would you cover for me? Tell him I'm out or something, then let me know and I'll call him back from here."

"Not a problem," Portia replied. "Relax and take care of yourself. You know I'm more than happy to do anything I can to help you do just that."

They said goodbye and hung up, Julia's thoughts turning to the task before her. She let her gaze sweep the terminal. Cruz had met her four times now and each time, she'd been unprepared. How would he appear in such a public place? Surely she'd see him coming.

She closed her eyes briefly. Four times? That was

all? Except for Tomas, she could hardly remember her life before Cruz had come into it, but their meetings repeated themselves with stunning detail. If she'd had a normal existence before, this might have bothered her, but she merely noted the detail and absorbed it. Only Tomas mattered.

She was going to help Cruz kill her husband and, in return, Cruz would give her and Tomas their freedom.

For one fleeting second she wondered what Mrs. Steelman, her childhood Sunday-school teacher back in Pascagoula, would think of that trade.

Julia decided she didn't give a damn what the woman would think. When Mrs. Steelman had experienced what Julia had, *then* she could express an opinion.

CRUZ STUDIED the terminal one more time, his attention landing again on the young mother with two children who'd caught his eye early on. She'd followed Julia to the seating area and had sat down three rows over, her stare bright and curious as she'd watched Julia. Was she simply admiring Julia's "Americanness" or was her attention being paid for by Ramirez?

Cruz's plans, ever fluid, took on a different shape. He dialed Julia's cell phone. It wasn't encrypted, but by the time Ramirez got the transcript the shit would already be on the fan.

Her expression turned to panic when her cell phone beeped. She dug it out of her purse and looked at it, and for a moment, Cruz didn't think she was going to answer. Finally she punched one of the buttons and lifted it to her ear. Her voice was guarded. *"Sí?"*

"Smile and act happy to hear my voice."

Her face changed so rapidly it took him by complete surprise. At the same time, she began to chatter at him in Spanish, the conversation inanely cheerful. Had she been an actress at one time, or was this another way she'd learned to cope with her life? He tried once again not to be impressed, but he failed.

"When we hang up, I want you to walk to the ladies' room at the other gate," he ordered. "The one south of where you are. There's a woman seated behind you who could be following you. I'm not sure, but I want to check her out before we do anything else. I'll call you back."

Julia wished him a happy birthday, told him she loved him, then said goodbye. A second later, she stood and headed in the direction he'd told her to go. He couldn't help but stare. Somewhere along the line, she'd learned to walk like a *chica* from South America, her hips swinging seductively, her shoulders held back, her breasts thrust forward. He could have watched her for hours, but he forced his eyes back to the woman with the children. She was studying Julia, too, but she did not get up. Pulling a bottle from the bag at her feet and then a stuffed toy, she turned her attention to the children.

Cruz gave her another ten minutes to move. She stayed exactly where she was so he dialed Julia again. "Don't return to your gate," he said. "Find the exit door between the two areas on the west side. Ignore the sign on the door. The alarm has been disabled. Wait until no one's near, then open it and go outside."

He ended the call before she could answer. Two minutes passed before she stepped out, almost into his arms. He dropped the night-vision binoculars he'd been using, took her elbow and drew her into the deeper shadows.

She didn't gasp or make any other sound. She'd been prepared this time and her only outward response to his presence was the widening of her eyes. Pressed together in the darkness, though, he felt her body react. Her muscles bunched beneath her skin as if she were about to take flight and once again he realized how strong she was.

"Whoa…" he said softly. "It's me…"

She exhaled slowly.

Cruz continued to hold her, mere inches separating his lips from hers. He had a lot of experience in closing that type of gap and this one was particularly tempting. Julia's lips were full and sensual and they didn't seem to go with the rest of her. As he thought this, though, he immediately wondered if he had things backward. Maybe the jittery aloofness that seemed to cushion her from the rest of the world was what didn't go. Julia had had to learn how to protect herself from the bastard. She could blend in, if necessary—her way of walking proved that, but maybe she'd preserved her soul by pulling into herself.

His better judgment took control before he could kiss her and find out. She deserved more respect than that. She was a woman on a mission and she was prepared to pay the price for success, no matter what it was. For that reason alone, he needed to keep his distance.

There was another reason, too, though, and this one meant even more, considering everything she'd gone through. Meredith had told Cruz exactly how Miguel Ramirez had abused Julia, physically and emotionally. Until she had time to recover, the last thing Julia needed was someone taking advantage of her.

She relaxed, but only slightly, her focus skipping to the binoculars then back to his face. "You were watching me through the window."

"I didn't want to go inside in case Ramirez had people there."

"Was the woman you saw one of his?"

"I don't think so. She didn't follow you."

They made no effort to move. His eyes locked on hers. "You made the arrangements with Portia?"

She nodded.

"Do you think she suspected anything?"

"No, not at all." She paused and he could feel her breathing. It had slowed a bit, but now it sped up. "But Guillermo's back. He brought me to the airport."

"And?"

She tensed again. "Do you think it's possible he could have been the man who attacked me?"

Her question didn't surprise Cruz, because he'd already considered the idea. "Anything's possible," he said, "but this isn't the time to discuss it. We should have left the minute you got here."

She nodded and started out from the overhang, but Cruz held her fast, disregarding his own warning. Confused by his hesitation, she stopped, her puzzled eyes meeting his.

"One more thing…"

"Yes?"

"We've only got one chance at this, Julia, and we can't make any mistakes. Don't talk, don't sneeze, don't even breath out loud," he warned. "And if we're caught…"

She waited.

"I want you to say I kidnapped you and you have no idea who I am."

"They'll kill you," she said bluntly. "It won't matter if the police or Miguel's men find us, once they hear that, you're a dead man."

"Let me worry about that," he advised. "You just look out for yourself."

"But Cruz—"

"Didn't you hear what I said, Julia? Don't do anything but stay quiet and do whatever I tell you to do. Those are the rules. If you can't follow them, let me know now and we'll stop right here."

She looked so deeply into his eyes that Cruz felt it in his heart. So many years had passed since anyone had touched him there he'd forgotten he even had one. The feeling was strange.

"I'm sick and tired of following someone else's rules," she said quietly. "This is a joint effort. Don't treat me as if I don't know what I'm doing because, as awful as it is, I understand Miguel's world better than you ever will."

He started to tell her how wrong she was. Julia knew exactly what Miguel Ramirez *wanted* her to know and absolutely nothing more.

In the end, Cruz didn't bother. Instead, he took her arm and moved out.

DESPITE THE APPEARANCE of the rickety truck Cruz led Julia to, they reached the edge of the mountains in record time, their headlights cutting dual beams through the darkness. Most of the trip passed in silence. Julia had no idea what might be on Cruz's mind, but as she stared blindly at the dirty windshield, all she could do was think about her confusion.

Cruz left her feeling so mixed up. Was it possible to be afraid of a man and attracted to him, too? Had her time with Miguel perverted her somehow? Would she ever be able to have a normal relationship with a normal man? Afraid to examine the questions too closely for fear of what they said about her, Julia concentrated on Cruz.

Something about him seemed to demand a physical response from her. Maybe her body was the only thing left she could trust. Her heart had betrayed her when she'd fallen for Miguel, so what else was left? The irony of that thought didn't go unnoticed. Miguel had won her heart then taken her body. Now, finding herself attracted to another man for the first time in years, it was her body she wanted to give him and her heart she protected.

Cruz spoke. "We've come almost a hundred klicks. We should be getting close to the road you're looking for."

She leaned forward, the dash lights bathing her face in green light as she checked the crude map she'd drawn for herself before leaving the compound. "Keep going," she said. "You're almost there, but we'll only have a few miles of road once you turn off."

He looked down at her sandals. "You have boots?"

"No," she said. "I thought I'd wing it in my Jimmy Choos."

He frowned and for the first time in a long time,

Julia allowed herself to laugh out loud. "Of course, I brought boots," she said, jerking a thumb over her shoulder. "They're in my bag along with the rest of my clothes."

Oblivious to the joke but clearly not caring, Cruz shrugged and continued to drive. A moment later, their lights illuminated a rough opening to the right of the highway. In the States, it would have been nothing more than a footpath but in South America it qualified as a road. A *good* road.

"That's it." With excitement, Julia pointed out the barely visible clearing. "Up there, straight ahead."

He slowed and steered the ancient truck on to the unpaved track. Julia grabbed for the cracked door handle at her right, but she wasn't fast enough. She slid across the seat and didn't stop until she hit Cruz's thigh.

He turned off the truck's lights and glanced at her. "You okay?"

She righted herself awkwardly and nodded. "I understand now why Miguel has an SUV with four-wheel drive. I thought it was vanity, but it's probably the only vehicle you could drive in all the way."

Cruz negotiated a sharp right then glanced at her. There was no moon, but she could see his expression in the ambient light. He looked curious as he asked her the same question Portia had the week before.

"Does it bother you to know your husband has a mistress?" he asked. "Considering everything, I find it hard to believe that it would, but I've never known a woman who wouldn't feel a least a twinge of jealousy at that kind of news."

"I don't care at all," she said. "I made a terrible mistake when I married Miguel and I blame no one for that except myself. I should have…" She paused and thought about her parents' vehement protests and how she'd ignored them. "I should have done a lot of things, but I thought I knew better. I married him, he turned out to be a monster, now I'm getting a chance to escape. The fact that he has a mistress is the least of my concerns. I just want my son and a normal life. That's it."

"You sound as if you blame yourself for everything that went wrong."

"I do."

"But doesn't Miguel bear some responsibility? He's the bad guy here."

The way he spoke made her think Cruz knew something about Miguel that she didn't. She looked at him thoughtfully. "That's true, but I fell for him," she said. "And I ignored all the advice I got to leave him alone. I think deep down I knew better."

"But you were in too far to pull back. And Miguel pressured you. He knew the right things to say and you thought you'd met the man of your dreams."

She couldn't ignore his accuracy this time. "How did you know?" she asked sharply.

"I've had a few illusions of my own interrupted over the years," he said. "Chalk it up to experience."

"I don't think so," she said slowly. "I think—"

He stopped the truck so abruptly Julia had to brace herself. With a speed she wouldn't have thought possible—by him or by the truck—Cruz reversed directions and yanked the wheel to his right. The vehicle plowed through a minuscule opening in the vegetation that Julia saw only as they went through it. A second later, the jungle swallowed them, including the noise of the truck's engine as Cruz switched it off. He smashed the truck's map light with a single punch, then he seized her arm and threw open the door. They both tumbled out of the truck and ran. Three or four seconds passed before Cruz dropped to the ground and pulled her down as well. In an instant, she found herself pressed against a carpet of undergrowth, Cruz's substantial weight on top of her. Several details registered—how he smelled, how he felt, how he sounded as he breathed into her ear.

"Don't move," he ordered. "Don't even think."

His request was easy to follow. In shock over the suddenness of his actions, she lay beneath him, her eyes screwed shut, her pulse racing. He'd thrown his arm down to cushion their fall and her cheek was pressed against it. She opened one eye halfway and stared. The hair that curled on his forearm was soft and black, the skin beneath it tanned.

She took a deep breath and he slipped his hand over the top of her head. Julia took it as a gesture of comfort until she realized he was covering up her hair. He didn't want it to betray their position.

They'd been motionless for ten minutes when Julia heard the first SUV pass. Five minutes later, another one followed.

They hid at least another half hour. When Cruz finally crawled off her, Julia wasn't sure she could stand. Her legs had gone numb from his weight. Gathering herself regardless, she stopped when Cruz held out his hand, palm down.

Stay there, he mouthed. *I'll be back.*

She sank back down in relief—her ego didn't want him to know how stiff she'd become—but instantly, she wished she'd gone with him. The quiet surrounded her and the darkness moved in closer, her memories coming with them. The last time she'd tried to run away, she'd spent a whole night in the jungle, lost and confused. She'd been terrified until Miguel's men had found her, then she'd learned real fear.

She thought she heard something to her left but before she could look, Cruz appeared. On her right.

He helped her up. "They're gone," he said, "but I don't want to risk using the truck again. I didn't expect to see anyone on this road, much less two vehicles. We'll walk from here. It's only ten miles."

In the darkness, Julia froze. "How do you know that? I only gave you directions to here."

He answered in a steady voice, his eyes on hers.

"You said we were ten miles away when I turned left, Julia. Don't you remember?"

"No, I don't," she said, confused. "I—I remember thinking about it, but I don't remember saying anything to you."

"Well, you did." He dropped the bags he'd retrieved from the truck. "I can do a lot, but I don't read minds. How else would I know?"

She stared at him blankly, his question echoing inside her mind. How else indeed?

"Change your clothes," he ordered. "We're heading out."

CHAPTER TEN

CRUZ LET Julia take the lead as they started down the path, Julia now dressed in jeans and boots, each of them carrying the backpacks Cruz had retrieved from the truck. With one slip of the tongue, he'd almost screwed up everything, but the two unexpected vehicles had made him jumpy. If he hadn't caught their headlights as they'd wound down the road above them, he and Julia would have been trapped right in the open. He was sure that Miguel had been in one of them, too. He needed to start paying attention to his job or he was the one who was going to get them both killed.

They'd been walking half an hour when Julia paused and looked at her topographical map using a small penlight. Stuffing it back into the pocket of her jeans, she adjusted her course to the right and continued. They were on a trail, if you could call it that, but she was smart enough to know she couldn't follow it blindly. The jungle was a cat that could change its spots. Vegetation grew overnight and an entire section of land, once well-known, could become foreign territory within hours. He'd seen experienced trackers get lost in Southeast Asia because they hadn't prepared well enough.

Julia didn't have that problem.

In fact, sometime between the truck and the track, they'd switched roles. Cruz knew exactly where it'd happened, too. When she'd moved ahead of him to lead the way, two distinct changes had come over her, one physical, one mental. He'd seen the physical difference in the purpose her stride had acquired and in the determined set of her shoulders. The mental he'd had to guess at, but it was just as real. She'd shed the skin of pampered wife and taken on the aura of a person with a mission.

She combined the elegant blonde *and* the determined mother and became something he couldn't name.

They continued in the dark for another two hours then Julia raised her hand and stopped them again. Wiping her forehead, she looked over her shoulder as he came even with her. "We'll take a ten-minute rest here," she said. "We ought to be getting close. We might be able to see their lights in another half hour or so."

Crouching, Cruz glanced down at the luminous dial of his watch. "It's almost one-thirty. By the time we get there, it'll be two-thirty, maybe three."

She finished his thought for him. "We can double

back and camp on the ridge just out of sight then go in tomorrow night and grab Tomas."

Cruz leaned against the tree behind him. "I'm surprised at you, Julia."

"Why is that?"

"I thought you'd want to rush in tonight. We're so close—it'll only be three when we get there. We'd still have plenty of darkness."

"We need more than just the dark." She shook her head. "This is probably a working farm. The laborers would be on their way in by four, definitely by five. We wouldn't have any room for mistakes. No, we need to go earlier. The guards will be sleepier right after they've eaten dinner and so will everyone else. I'd say we hit it about this time—one-thirty or so."

"How do you know it's a farm?" he asked casually.

"That's all that's in the area."

"Are you sure?"

She glared at him. "Don't you remember what I told you? I do my homework. The mistakes I made last time taught me there's no such thing as being too prepared."

Cruz let the issue drop. He didn't want her knowing what he knew. The less said the better.

Julia must have felt the same way. She finished the bottle of water she'd been drinking, rose from the tree stump where she'd been sitting and lifted her backpack. "Let's go."

Cruz followed without a word.

A half hour later, Cruz was the one who stopped. With a hiss only Julia could hear, he motioned her to halt. She dropped down and waited for him to approach.

"What is it?"

"I heard something," he said.

"It's too soon to be there," she argued. "Maybe it was an animal—"

He laid two fingers across her lips and she fell silent. Slithering off the path, Cruz took her with him. "Wait here," he said. "I'll be back."

She started to protest but he silenced her with a look. Disappearing into the thick undergrowth, Cruz continued forward, parallel to the path they'd been on. A few meters on, he heard voices.

At the same time, something rustled in the thick undergrowth behind him.

He slowed his heart rate, took a single breath, then pivoted.

His arm was around Julia's throat before he knew it was her. When her identity sank in, it was too late for him to stop. He had her off the ground and his hand was against her head, preparing to snap her neck. Somehow he managed to pull back.

Clawing at his fingers, Julia kicked him the shins. If she'd had the breath to do so, she would have screamed. Anger exploding inside him at her disobedience, Cruz increased the pressure of his forearm against her windpipe.

His mouth moved against her ear. "Do—not—speak." He shook her slightly and let his hold ease minutely. "Understood?"

He waited until she nodded, then he turned her to face him and their eyes locked. She saw his anger and cringed, making him almost regret showing it. Almost.

He let her down slowly, her body sliding the length of his until her feet touched the ground.

Regardless of his warning, she opened her mouth, but then she froze, her lips forming into an *O* of fright as she finally heard what he had.

There were two of them and they were speaking Spanish. Cruz noted their accent and their vocabulary. They were locals.

"*Sí, sí, chico,*" the first man was saying. "You may think you're smart, but my dog has more brains in his dick than you do in your head…"

The second man laughed, the sound high and youthful. "You're jealous, old man. You want a woman like mine so you compare me to your dog! Let me tell you…"

Cruz caught a glimpse of the men. They wore boots and jungle camo, their faces blackened as well as their hands. Each had a TEC-9 strung across their chest. They disappeared into the jungle a moment later, their voices finally fading. They had no idea how close to death they'd walked.

Julia looked up Cruz. "We must be closer than I thought."

"No shit," he answered dryly.

SHE DIDN'T KNOW which mistake bothered her more.

As Julia and Cruz searched for a vantage point above the villa, she cursed herself for making both of them. One would cost them time and the other had almost cost her her life.

She'd studied her topo maps so much before leaving that she'd ignored her instincts. Consequently she'd been off by one ridge. Way before Cruz had heard the two guards, she'd begun to get nervous, a hot looseness developing in the pit of her stomach. She'd chalked the reaction up to being so close to Cruz but, in reality, her gut had been trying to warn her. She needed to pay closer attention to where they actually were and use the maps with more caution.

Creeping up behind Cruz had been the bigger mistake, though. She should have stayed put, like he'd ordered. She put her hand against her neck. Another few seconds and a little more pressure and he would have killed her. The reality shook her deeply but at the same time, it was strangely reassuring to know she was with a man that deadly. There was no question in her mind that he could take care of her and Tomas.

Her stupidity had angered him, though. Except for a few brief expletives, Cruz had said nothing else since the men had left. Walking before her with a digital monitor of some sort, he ignored her, moving so deliberately it felt as if they were going in slow motion. Eventually he stopped and pulled her to his side. He was drenched in sweat and so was she. He pointed to his eyes then to the valley below.

She looked down as instructed. A surprisingly modest villa sat in the center of a small clearing, the home's white stucco gleaming in the moonlight. A pool was on one side, the shimmering oval of water motionless. There were palm trees around the perimeter of the garden area, but little else. No one would be able to approach the home without being seen.

Julia's heart thumped painfully as she took out her binoculars and studied the windows across the front of the house. Which one separated her from her precious child? Was he sleeping peacefully? Did he miss her as much as she missed him?

She didn't realize she was crying until a tear slid down her cheek. Brushing at it angrily, she caught Cruz's attention. His gaze seemed to harden but she wasn't sure and she didn't care. She met his eyes unflinchingly. To hell with him. He could think what he liked. She'd gotten them this far when, without her, he wouldn't have known where to begin.

They lay in the dark for an hour. Cruz stayed so still and quiet Julia couldn't tell if he was breathing. Even his gaze, like a lizard's in the sun, seemed fixed and steady. It wasn't, though. He was counting the guards that came in and out of view and studying the house itself, filing the information away. She couldn't guess what he saw or how he knew to look for certain things.

A lot of questions had tormented her in the days since Cruz had shown up but Julia had come to believe one thing. Meredith *had* probably sent him to help Julia. But that didn't mean she'd sent him to kill Miguel. Why would she want that? Someone else was involved in this, but who? Living with Miguel had taught her to be suspicious. She had to protect herself, and knowing the answer to that mystery was essential.

After another thirty minutes, Cruz tilted his head behind them, then indicated she should follow.

"Hook your hands in my belt and don't step anywhere but in my tracks," he whispered. "I've been checking but I could have missed something. This area's been mined."

Now she understood the monitor. Julia swallowed nervously but did exactly as he instructed. It seemed to take them an hour to return to the spot they'd picked as their camp but in reality, less than twenty minutes passed. As it was, Cruz had to point out the lean-to he'd set in place after the guards had passed. Hidden between two huge fallen trees, the leafy net blended so well with the vegetation behind it that she would have missed the shelter without him.

She climbed beneath the cover and shook out one of the sleeping mats with a long sigh. Her weariness went beyond anything she'd felt before and she guessed it had as much to do with her mental state as physical exhaustion.

Cruz had followed her in and now he glared at her in the darkness. His expression told her he'd kept his feelings to himself as long as he could.

"If you do that again—" his voice sounded like faraway thunder that was slowly moving in "—I'm turning around and leaving you here."

"It was a mistake!"

"I'm not talking about the ridge," he said. "You deliberately followed me after I told you to stay put."

"I'd looked at the map," she protested. "I wanted to warn you that I'd screwed up—"

"I don't give a rat's ass what you wanted to tell me. It's a miracle we're not both lying under a tree with our guts spilling from bullet holes."

"I didn't know they were there—"

"Exactly!" he said with mounting frustration. "You didn't but I *did.* That's why I told you to stay behind. We can't afford a mistake like that."

His criticism rankled, especially because she knew he was right. "I don't want to listen to this right now," she said. "I just want to rest, and tomorrow I want to get my son back. When it's over, you can sue me for the mistake, okay?"

She started to turn over, but he stopped her. "I don't think you understand," he said ominously.

"I understand perfectly." She tried to jerk away from his grip but he wouldn't let go.

"No," he answered. "You don't. But you're going to."

He pulled something from the backpack he'd been carrying. When he turned to face her once more, her mouth dropped open.

He held a braided rope.

"Put your hands together," he ordered.

Dumbfounded, Julia looked at him. "Are you insane? I'm not going to let you tie me up."

"I don't trust you, Julia." He reached behind her and grabbed her other arm, looping the rope between her wrists too quickly for her to react. "There's nothing to keep you from slipping out of here and trying to go in there on your own." He tightened the knot then met her eyes. "Except this."

"That's not true," she said. "There *is* something else."

"And it is?"

"My word," she answered. "I promised you my help in return for your own. I don't go back on my word."

"That's nice." With a dismissive expression, he wrapped the other end of the rope around his hand, stretched out on the mat beside her then rolled to his side. He spoke over his shoulder. "Really nice. But I still don't trust you, so go to sleep, Julia, and don't think about leaving. I might not be as slow the second time I try to kill you."

MORNING CAME sooner than Julia expected, the noise and movement of the jungle waking her as dawn arrived. Lying on her back, she opened her eyes and realized that her whole body ached. She hurt in places she didn't even know muscles existed, but worse the mental weariness she'd felt last night had not abated. Waiting for the day to pass, waiting for Cruz to arrive, waiting for the discovery she'd prayed wouldn't happen… Yesterday had been a day to wait and today was going to be even worse.

But who cared?

By this time tomorrow, she would have her son.

The thought lifted her heart and she actually smiled.

Cruz's voice sounded softly in her ear. "You ought to do that more often."

She turned her head. Like two lovers who'd spent the night together, their faces were a breath apart. Up close, his eyes looked darker, the wall he maintained between himself and the outside world slipping away for a moment to reveal more than he usually allowed. Julia glimpsed inside then she pulled back. She wasn't ready to know all his secrets and she didn't think she ever would be.

"Do what more often?" she said, regaining her senses.

"Smile like that," he answered lazily. "You look completely different when you smile."

"Different how?"

He raised himself on his elbow then propped his head on his fist. He touched her temple with his other hand. "For one thing, you're aren't frowning." He rubbed his finger across her forehead. "No wrinkles."

She shivered. "What else?"

"Well…"

He lengthened the word to four syllables and she laughed, deepening her Southern accent when she spoke. "You keep talking like that, somebody's gonna accuse you of comin' from Pascagoula."

"There are worse places to be from," he said.

"You couldn't have convinced me of that when I was seventeen," she replied. "I couldn't wait to leave. I wanted a life—a *real* life like I thought Meredith had lived—and I left for college the minute I could. I was so naive."

He looked at her with speculation in his eyes. "Aren't you supposed to be naive when you're young?"

"Not like that. I didn't have a clue of what the world was actually like and I was totally unprepared. My parents kept me way too protected. I want my son to be able to care for himself. It's going to be hard enough for him to grow up without a father, I don't want him disadvantaged in that department, too.

He took her wrists and untied her, dropping the

rope between them. "I grew up without a father," he said matter-of-factly. "Or a mother."

"Oh, Cruz…" Julia reached out and touched his arm then realized what she'd done. She pulled her hand back awkwardly. What was she thinking? "I'm so sorry. What happened?"

"I never knew either one of them." He lay back on his mat and stared at the netting above them, his voice so quiet she had to strain to hear him. "I was left at a hospital in Mexico City when I was just a baby. The nuns took pity on me and, instead of turning me over to the orphanage down the street, I became their pet. I lived inside the hospital until I was twelve."

Cruz's voice held no emotion whatsoever and the very lack of it made Julia understand him better than anything he'd disclosed about himself—on purpose or inadvertently—since she'd met him.

"Were you adopted then?" she asked hopefully.

He smiled at her question, his expression clearly saying she hadn't yet lost all her naiveté. "I was kicked out," he answered. "A new abbess took over, and I went out the door with the trash she didn't want. I lived on the street after that."

"All alone?"

"There are hundreds—thousands—of kids in Mexico City who live that way, Julia. I was far from alone."

"But you were twelve." Julia stared at him in shock. "What did you do?"

"Anything I had to in order to survive. Anything," he repeated for emphasis, "and that includes everything."

The silence between them built until a macaw cried out overhead.

"There were younger ones than me out there. Hell, I was almost the old man *en la pandilla.* By the time I was sixteen, I was *El Jefe.*"

Julia put a hand to her throat, unable to say anything.

"Then I ended up back at the hospital, this time as a patient. Gang life is bad for your health."

She was almost afraid to ask but she had to know. "What happened?" she whispered.

"A knife found its way between my ribs." He rolled sideways and pulled up his shirt. His stomach looked as hard as a plate of steel. The ragged scar that bisected it revealed the truth, though. He was made of flesh and bone.

She ran her finger over the ragged line. "Does it still hurt?"

He seemed surprised at her question. "Yes, actually, it does sometimes. When I'm in a place where it's cold and wet, the muscle aches."

"My father had an accident with a pruning saw when I was a kid," she said with a knowing nod. "He used to complain about it in the winter."

"A pruning saw?" He appeared skeptical. "Who

would have thought a pruning saw could make a scar like that?"

"My mother and I went shopping and when we got home, the hospital called. A neighbor had brought him in after he'd fallen out of a tree with it in his hand. My mother was livid. I'm surprised she didn't kill him right then and there."

"The joys of marriage," he said.

Julia laughed lightly. "Yeah, it's one fun ride, that's for sure." She paused. "I take it you've never walked down the aisle?"

"No. My job isn't exactly conducive to relationships."

"What about before?"

"That wasn't any before," he answered flatly. "While I was in the hospital, I met a U.S. Marine who'd been unlucky enough to have an appendicitis attack while he was in Mexico. He had a friend, who had a friend, who had a friend…" His voice died off and he shrugged. "I worked alone for years then I hooked up with the organization I'm in and I've been there ever since."

This was the point to which Julia had wanted to bring him.

"And this organization," she started. "I don't think I understand it too well. Do you work for the government or for individuals?"

He stared at her blankly.

Licking her lips, she tried again. "I've heard of

governments using the kinds of services you provide, but Miguel has had everyone up to members of the presidential cabinet in our house. I can't image the Colombians would want him gone. And he's small fry to the U.S. government, I would think."

Again, Cruz said nothing.

"Who hired you?" Her voice was soft but her words were blunt. "I have a right to know who's paying you to kill my husband. How complicated is that question?"

When he didn't reply the third time, her frustration peaked. "Cruz, I asked you a simple question—"

"No, you didn't." He sat up abruptly. "It's a question that's anything *but* simple."

"All right, then," she said. "Give me the complicated answer."

"Forget it. Knowing the answer to that question is the quickest way I can think of to get you killed."

"But, Cruz—"

"But nothing." He stood and extended his hand. She accepted it reluctantly, allowing him to pull her to her feet. They stood side by side under the netting, closer than was necessary and much closer than she would have liked. "I'm not telling you who hired me, Julia. And by the way," he added softly, "Miguel Ramirez is not really your husband. Your marriage to him is not legal and it never has been."

CHAPTER ELEVEN

JULIA'S EXPRESSION DIDN'T change and, for a second, Cruz wasn't sure she had heard him. He'd needed a diversion and this information had been the best that he could do. Had it worked or had he put her in shock?

Finally she spoke, her words very deliberate, her diction precise. "What did you say?"

He gave a silent sigh of relief that he'd distracted her. "Your marriage to Miguel Ramirez isn't legal. The man who performed the ceremony in the Bahamas was someone Ramirez paid to act out the part. The papers you signed weren't real."

She closed her eyes briefly then opened them. "We applied for a marriage license at the courthouse in Nassau. I saw the documents. They had a governmental stamp on them. They were legitimate."

"The 'minister' wasn't a minister and the documents were never officially registered because they weren't real."

Her face seemed to crumple and he feared she might as well, her reaction surprising him. She didn't love the son of a bitch. Cruz had thought she would have been happy to find out she wasn't tied to him.

Without another word she stepped from under the netting into the dappled sunlight. He stuffed the rope into his backpack then followed her outside. Five minutes passed before she spoke again. She kept her back to him.

"How do you know this?" she asked.

"I research my target, Julia. For weeks, I've been learning everything I could about Miguel. That meant finding out about his personal life, too. I went to the hotel in Nassau where you stayed and I talked to the people there. I didn't expect them to remember him but he spent so much money, the manager was able to recall him. I followed up what they told me by checking out the documentation myself." He took her by the shoulders and gently turned her around. "It was all a farce, Julia. Nothing about the rite was lawful."

"Why?"

The heartache in that single word grabbed Cruz and refused to let go. His expression stoic, he looked her straight in the eye and lied. "I don't know why, Julia," he said.

And then he pulled her to him.

Her resistance was only momentary and when it passed, she held on to him like someone who'd grabbed the last line to the last lifeboat. Cruz responded by holding her closer. Miguel Ramirez deserved to die for a lot of reasons, not the least of which, Cruz suddenly decided, was the pain he'd put in this woman's eyes.

Cruz kept her in the circle of his embrace until she leaned back to look at him but he didn't completely release her. He couldn't, it seemed.

"How could he do this to me?" she whispered, her eyes swimming. "I hate him now but I didn't then. I *loved* him. And he said he *loved* me. I don't understand."

Cruz had met dozens of men like Miguel Ramirez. They were bullies who weren't able to confront their enemies head-on so instead they used proxies to punish them. In Julia's case, the method he'd chosen to inflict his pain was somewhat imaginative, but there was nothing special about him. He was just another thug.

If he told her even that much, though, she'd have more questions and he couldn't give her the answers. They'd go with him to his grave, along with a few million other secrets he had.

"I don't understand, either." With those words, Cruz lied again. "But it doesn't matter, Julia. His days are numbered."

He could tell by her expression she wasn't satisfied, but she nodded slowly, then her gaze fell. Expecting her to step out of his embrace, Cruz waited for the hollow feeling he knew would follow, but she surprised him once again. She laid her head on his chest and held on.

He wondered if she could hear his heart.

Warnings rang out inside him. He was about to make a terrible mistake. He could jeopardize everything. He would regret this for the rest of his life. He called himself a few choice expletives, then he did exactly what he'd known all along he was going to do.

He lifted Julia's chin and kissed her.

She seemed to melt within his arms, any last thoughts she might have mustered fading under the demands of his mouth. He teased her lips apart with his tongue and then he deepened their kiss, bringing her body closer to his. Beneath his hands, the muscles in her hips flexed as she pushed herself upward to meet him, her breasts pressing against his chest.

For a second, Cruz let himself imagine what it would be like. He thought about taking off her clothing and touching her bare skin. He thought about running his hands along her curves and kissing every part of her.

Then he thought about the consequences.

He put his hands on her shoulders and gently forced her down. "We can't do this, Julia." His voice was hoarse with desire. "We can't."

She blinked. Her eyes were so blue Cruz felt as if he could dive into their depths and never return.

"Yes, we can," she said, surprising him once again. "You're not married and neither am I."

He tugged at her arms, but she wouldn't release him. "That's not the reason it'd be a mistake."

"Then what is?"

He made up his answer on the spot but as he spoke, he realized what he said was as much the truth as anything else. "You don't really want to make love. You're hurt and confused and worried so you want to make it all go away for a little while. That's not good enough. You need a better rationale than that for having sex."

"Like what?"

Once again, he said the first thing that came into his mind. "How about love?"

Her lips parted and the trees overhead stilled as if they were waiting, along with Cruz, to hear what she had to say. "I don't believe in love anymore," she whispered. "It doesn't exist."

Cruz could feel her body trembling as she spoke.

"That's not true and you don't believe it, either," he said. "Real love doesn't go anywhere. It lives in your heart and you carry it around with you. Even when the person you love isn't there anymore, the love still is."

"That sounds really good, Cruz. Very pretty, in fact." Her eyes filled up. "But you're lying, and you and I both know it."

CRUZ HAD BROUGHT MREs, and they ate the dehydrated food directly from the pouches, the silence between them heavy. Still reeling from his news that she wasn't really married, Julia felt more battered and beat-up than she had when she'd first woken that morning. Was there no end to Miguel's inexplicable cruelty? Nothing he'd done to her made any sense. Why hadn't she been able to see through him? How could she have been so blind?

She would *never* trust her emotional judgment again. She couldn't afford to make that kind of mistake twice in her lifetime and the only way she could avoid it for sure was not to even try.

All she had to do was think about Cruz if she needed further proof. The minute he'd pulled back after their kiss she'd known he was right to stop them. They had no business doing what they had, much less seeing it through to the end, but all Julia had wanted to do was lose herself in his arms and forget about what was happening, the mental turmoil too much for her to handle.

"Are you finished with that?" He nodded at the half-full package in her hand.

"Y-yes," she stuttered. "Yes, I am."

He collected her meal, along with his own leftovers, and stuffed everything into his backpack. No one would know they'd been there, much less spent the night.

Julia rummaged around in her own pack, then removed a small plastic bag that contained the few personal items she had brought. "I saw a stream about half a klick that way." She stood and tilted her head to the east. "I'll be right back."

Cruz rose as well. "I'll go with you."

"I'd like some privacy." Her voice was cool.

"And I'd like a cold beer," he said, "but neither one's gonna happen. I'm coming with you."

"Do you really think I'm stupid enough to try and grab Tomas in broad daylight? All by myself?"

"'Stupid' is the last word I'd use to describe you, Julia," he said. "But this isn't about trust. Those guards we saw yesterday are going to be back this morning. I'd just as soon you didn't run into them. I can keep an eye out while you clean up."

She wasn't sure she believed him, but she conceded the point with a nod. She turned to the path, but Cruz stopped her before she managed a single step and took the lead himself. Moving ahead of her with a silence that didn't seem possible, he took them directly to the stream she'd mentioned. His eyes never stopped searching the undergrowth that surrounded them.

"Go ahead," Cruz whispered. "But don't take too long."

Julia followed his instructions and went about her business as quickly as she could. She only paused once. Removing her tank top to wipe herself with water dipped from the stream, she felt Cruz's stare touch her back. She couldn't keep from turning and their eyes met over her bare shoulder. The look couldn't have lasted for more than a single heartbeat, but it left Julia thoroughly shaken. If there had been any question in her mind about whether or not Cruz wanted her, it was seared away by the heat in his gaze. He'd prevented them from making love, but he'd done so with difficulty. She wasn't proud of it, but a small satisfaction rippled over her.

She finished then slipped to his side. They returned to their camp in silence and the waiting began.

CRUZ PAID the price for his mistake with stoic acceptance. He'd known when he'd pulled Julia to him that something would happen but he'd proceeded regardless. Then *she'd* pressed *him* to go further. Stopping her was the last thing he'd thought he'd have to do— stopping himself had been his only worry.

He knew he'd done the right thing, but there was no satisfaction in that.

Time slowed then seemed to still completely, the jungle growing silent as the day's heat built. The interval didn't bother Cruz—he was a patient man, accustomed to waiting. Sitting quietly under their net, he studied the notes he'd already made on Amalia Riveria's house. He had the floor plan memorized, but there were details he wanted to make sure he had right. The only time he moved was when he left Julia at evenly spaced intervals to check their perimeter.

Julia wasn't nearly as calm. She was ready for action. Under the cover of their camouflage net, she paced with the restless agitation of a caged cat and muttered softly to herself. By early afternoon, she'd managed to infect him with her nervousness and he wasn't pleased. With himself or with her.

He thought about tying her up and putting some tape over her mouth, but instead he pulled out two more MREs, thinking a meal might distract her.

It did, but only momentarily. She finished first then stared at him. "What time do you want to go in?" she asked after a moment.

"You suggested one-thirty last night," he reminded her. "That's as good as anything."

"I don't think we should wait that long," she said. "What if…" Her words died out.

"What if what?" he asked.

Instead of answering, she looked down at her hands. She had them in her lap and she'd been twisting her fingers restlessly. She got control of herself and spoke, raising her eyes to his. "What if Tomas doesn't want to come with us?"

Cruz looked at her in surprise. "Why would you even worry about that? Every kid wants his mother. I'm sure he isn't any different."

"He isn't, but Miguel is so strange," she answered. "He could have told Tomas anything about me and no one would correct him. It'd be two against one," she said bitterly. "I can't imagine Amalia defending me."

"What did Portia say about her when you asked?"

Julia narrowed her eyes. "How do you know I asked her?"

"It only makes sense that you would."

"Portia confirmed everything that you had told me. She only added one piece of information and that was the fact that Amalia is very beautiful."

Remembering her reaction to his earlier news, Cruz hesitated before asking his next question. Every time he thought he had Julia figured out, she proved him wrong. "Does that bother you?"

"The only thing that matters to me is that she has Tomas." Julia's expression turned fierce. "He is *my* son and she has no right to him. She must be crazy to be with Miguel, but she's insane if she thinks she's going to raise my child. *I* am his mother and *I* will do that."

The conversation died with that, but Julia's nervous anxiety seemed to expire with it, the simple act of expressing her determination again apparently enough to calm her. Cruz resumed his own activities but kept one eye on her. If her disquiet returned, he'd have to confront her about it—emotions led to mistakes. She had to be focused.

The sun slipped behind the brush and dark fell suddenly. They couldn't risk a fire or light of any sort so they sat quietly. In the canopy overhead, the sounds grew louder. The animals were more active when the sun went down, but Cruz had always felt the lack of light amplified their cries as well. What was white noise during the day turned into frightful screeches after night arrived.

He spoke softly. "You should try and get some sleep. After we grab Tomas, we'll need to return to San Isidro as quickly as possible."

"I can't sleep," she said. "No way."

"You need to rest." He nodded toward the rear of the net. "Lay down and try. You might surprise yourself."

She didn't answer but, with his eyes finally adjusted to the lack of light, Cruz watched as Julia crawled on her hands and knees to a spot deeper under the net. He heard the mats rustle and then she sighed. After a bit, her breathing slowed and became deeper. He assumed she'd fallen asleep, but then she spoke softly.

"Cruz?"

He twisted halfway around. She was curled up right behind him, so close they were almost touching. "Yeah?"

Her voice sounded small in the darkness. "Thank you for helping me."

He stopped himself from touching her but just barely. "You're welcome," he said instead. Turning back to the opening in the net, he stared into the night, resuming his watch.

HOLDING HER ARMS OPEN, Julia cried out for Tomas, but her son acted as if he didn't see her and Miguel came out of nowhere to pick him up. They disappeared from view, the shadow of a woman with long black hair walking beside them....

Julia opened her eyes in confusion. Cruz was tugging gently on her shoulder, and tears still wet her cheeks.

"You were having a nightmare." He rubbed her face with his thumb, wiping away the evidence. In the darkness, his expression looked sympathetic, but Julia knew she was imagining things.

She sat up groggily. "What time is it?"

"It's getting close to one," he answered. "I wanted to wait a bit before I woke you but when you started crying, I went ahead. You were getting too loud."

"I was dreaming that Tomas wouldn't come to me. It was awful. Miguel was there and a woman was with him." She looked up at him, a catch coming into her throat to thicken her voice. "They took Tomas away."

"That's not going to happen."

They were sitting side by side, but Cruz leaned closer and took her chin between his fingers. She knew he did that because he wanted to make his point but his action had the opposite effect on her. Instead of drawing her attention to his words, it made her even more conscious of his nearness.

He looked directly into her eyes and she shivered.

"I'm going to get your son, Julia. I promised you I would and I keep my promises." He paused. "Just like I expect you to."

He studied her face for a moment before releasing her and turning to his backpack. She didn't realize she'd been holding her breath until she exhaled.

When he faced her again, he had a small jar in his left hand. He opened it and began to paint her face with a sticky black substance. When he finished, his hand lingered against the side of her face.

"You look like a cover model..." he teased "...for *Soldier of Fortune.*"

His unexpected joke eased the tension she felt.

"Do they pay well?" she asked. "I'm gonna need a job when this is over and I get back to the States."

"I don't know," he confessed. "I'll find out and get back to you on that. I have friends in high places who should know."

"I bet you do have those kinds of friends," she said thoughtfully.

He stowed the jar and removed a piece of paper, the time for banter quickly over. Squatting, he flattened out the paper on the mat between them.

"This is supposed to be a plan of Riveria's house." He tapped one corner with his finger. "I'm pretty sure Tomas sleeps in this bedroom, at least that's what I've been told. Next to his room is where the nanny stays. If he's asleep, will she be in her own room or in his?"

Julia looked in amazement at the crude drawing. "Where did you get this?"

He waved aside her question with impatience. "A cop owed me a favor. But it doesn't matter, Julia, just answer the question."

"Miguel didn't take our usual woman so Mari's not there, but someone would be nearby, that's for sure." She bit her bottom lip. "If Tomas is sleeping and there *is* a nanny, my guess is she'll be in her own room. There would be no need for her to be right beside him unless he was sick or something."

"That's what I thought, too." Cruz pointed to the other corner of the house. "When he's there, Miguel sleeps here, as does Amalia. In the corridor between the two rooms, a single guard is supposedly stationed. I counted three yesterday, so that means there's at least that many, maybe more if I missed some."

Julia frowned. "That doesn't sound right, Cruz. Miguel is a security nut. He'd have more men around him than that."

"In San Isidro, yes, but not here. He thinks no one knows about this place, Julia. It's his getaway. His sanctuary. I was sure he was in one of those SUVs we saw, but you never know."

"What about Amalia?"

Jimenez had been less than helpful about Riveria's whereabouts. "I don't know," Cruz answered truthfully. "I was told she comes and goes a lot. If they were here, either one of them—or both for that matter—could have been in the vehicles we saw leaving yesterday. We need to be prepared for any possibility."

She took the information in stride. "Okay. Go on."

"This time of night, the guards will be in the dining room where they congregate after eating." He paused. "I'm not going to try and take them down. All I want is a silent snatch and run. My plan is to slip in through the window, grab Tomas, then jump back out."

She let his words soak in, then she asked quietly. "Do you have a gun I can use? Miguel keeps everything locked up and I couldn't risk taking something—"

"I don't use weapons. They make noise, they draw attention, and they leave messes. I prefer to handle things on my own."

She'd been frowning as he spoke, but suddenly she understood and, with that comprehension, a flash of fear came. She remembered his hand on her neck.

Her stomach spasming in nervousness, Julia asked, "And what do I do while you're doing this?"

Dark eyes on hers, he said, "I'll explain that when we get closer."

His planning seemed impeccable. Anxious to start and get the whole thing behind her, Julia got to her feet.

Cruz held her backpack, and she slipped her arms inside the loops. Gathering his own pack, he did the same and they stepped out from under the shelter into the rustling darkness. Cruz gave a hard yank to a rope along the edge of the netting and the whole thing sank with a poof onto the ground where it instantly blended in. He shuffled a few leaves on top of it then took off down the path. Julia stayed on his heels and watched where he walked, the mines he'd mentioned yesterday still fresh in her thoughts.

Even though it was now familiar, the trail looked sinister to Julia as they walked it. The vegetation along the edge seemed to have crept closer in twenty-four hours and even the wild bougainvillea and bird-of-paradise, so beautiful before, seemed menacing. As they went through a heavily grown area, a monkey screeched overhead. Startled by the sound, Julia glanced up and a branch on an Aguano caught her attention. When the twig moved again, she understood why she'd noticed it—it wasn't part of the tree. It was a snake, as big around as her arm. He hissed a silent warning. She closed her eyes and shuddered but when she looked again, she saw nothing but a limb.

Within twenty minutes, they were at the ridge where they'd been the day before. She thought she heard music, but Julia dismissed the ridiculous idea as quickly as it came. Who would be playing a stereo in the middle of the jungle at this time of night? She wouldn't have given it a second thought in the city but out here? Her stress was getting to her, she decided, because she was so close to success. Everything she'd worked for, everything she wanted, it had all come down to this and she could almost taste her freedom.

Sinking into the vegetation underneath a huge rubber tree twenty feet from their previous spot, Cruz motioned her down beside him.

The house looked exactly like it had the night before, except for one big difference.

The place was full of people. There were so many of them, they had spilled from inside the dimly lit home to the patio. Everyone held a glass of something and many of them were dancing, some even out on the grass. A rowdy flock of children played on a wooden gym set near the edge of a clearing that hadn't been there the day before.

Julia stared in disbelief while, beside her, Cruz cursed softly.

CHAPTER TWELVE

AFTER HIS MUTTERED DAMN, Cruz allowed himself no further reaction. Instead, he began to reassess the situation, his mind shifting through a list of possibilities, discarding each one almost as quickly as it came to him. They couldn't leave and return another time—a second absence by Julia wouldn't go unnoticed and, besides that, Ramirez was moving too fast with his own activities to postpone anything. Hell, they couldn't even wait until the party was over. It'd be daylight by then. Cruz considered a dozen other scenarios but none of them felt right.

Cruz was slipping on his night-vision goggles when Julia's voice broke into his thoughts.

"He's there," she breathed. "Oh, my gosh, Cruz! Tomas is right down there." She dropped the binoculars she'd yanked from her pack to point to the children by the swing set. "Look!"

Cruz did as she instructed. He'd seen countless photos of Tomas before any of this had even begun and in addition, once he'd arrived, he'd watched the little boy play in the compound. "I see him." Staring at the child, a plan began to take shape. It wasn't one Cruz would have considered unless it was necessary, but the more he thought about it, the more convinced he became that it might actually work. He watched Tomas tackle another child harmlessly on the grass. Cruz slid his goggles upward.

He expected to see distress, but Julia's face revealed an entirely different emotion. Her cheeks were colored with excitement, the gleam in her dark eyes too bright to miss.

"This is perfect," she whispered before he could say a thing. "You couldn't have asked for better."

Cruz wouldn't have described the situation that way, but he waited to see what she had to say. Her inborn sense of strategy continued to surprise him, even though he knew she came by it naturally. He decided to test her.

"Have you lost your mind?" He tilted his head toward the house. "How the hell am I going to get in there now? Don't you think someone might notice? Look at all those people."

"I have," she said. "And I've counted them, too. There's between sixty and a hundred of them and no one's patrolling, either. All you have to do is walk up and join the party, Cruz." She pulled up the tail of her shirt and started rubbing the makeup off her face, nodding toward him to indicate he should do the same. "Miguel doesn't know you! You could go right up to Tomas and grab him and no one will think a thing."

Her face now clear of the camouflage paint, she was studying the milling crowd, which was how she missed Cruz's look of amazement. She'd just suggested the very thing he'd decided on doing. Presented with an identical problem, most people he knew would have thrown their hands in the air and given up.

"You're nuts," he said, to cover his surprise.

"No, I'm not!" she argued. "It's a great plan."

Cruz lowered his goggles and scanned the crowd one more time.

"Something's not right," he said, almost to himself. "Something's wrong. What is it? What's out of sync?"

Not expecting any kind of answer, he continued to mutter then Julia spoke, her voice holding the puzzlement he felt. "This is hard to believe," she said, dropping her glasses to look at him. "You must have incredible luck."

"What is it?" he asked, his skin prickling.

"Those people down there..." She gestured toward the house. "They aren't friends of Miguel's. They're uniformed. They're his employees." Her eyes rounded as the consequences of what she'd said became clear. Her voice revealed her wonderment, as if she couldn't believe that anyone who worked for Miguel would take such a risk. "He's not there, Cruz. He's not there and they're having a party."

Julia had put her finger exactly on what had bothered him.

Was it luck? Or a setup?

The two black SUVs they'd hid from the day before came back into Cruz's mind. Ramirez and Amalia could have been in either one of them or they could have been filled with decoys.

Julia's voice distracted him. "They've got a couple of teenagers watching the kids. I don't see anyone who looks like a nanny. They're all drinking, too." She turned and stared at Cruz, her fingers gripping her binoculars so tightly her knuckles gleamed white. "They're not paying any attention to those children, Cruz. They're so drunk they don't even know where *they* are, much less what the kids are doing. They'll never miss one."

Cruz didn't waste any more time. He leaned closer to Julia and began to tell her what they were going to do.

JULIA FELT as if her heart had leaped into her throat and lodged there. She couldn't catch her breath and her pulse was going so fast, her body must have thought she was in a race.

Tomas was six feet away from where she now hid.

Screened from view by the thick undergrowth, Julia pushed herself another foot closer, her anticipation building even more as she watched her son. Had he grown in two weeks? Was he well? Was he happy? The answer to all three questions appeared to be yes, but until she had him in her arms, Julia wouldn't know for sure. She remembered the day she'd given birth. Like every new mother, she'd counted his toes and fingers, examining him from top to bottom. She wanted to do the same thing again.

And in another ten minutes, she could.

Julia glanced at the crowd again. She was confident in her assessment of who they really were. Some even wore uniforms she recognized. Miguel liked to have the people around him, especially those who were working for him, to look a certain way. In San Isidro, his housekeepers were required to dress completely in white, as well as the men who worked in the yard. The security guards wore tan slacks and black, short-sleeved shirts. She picked out the same uniforms here and the people who wore them seemed to fit those roles.

A shriek came from one of the children as he kicked a soccer ball toward Tomas, and Julia checked her watch. Two more minutes. Relaxing the muscles in her legs, Julia concentrated on staying focused. That had been Cruz's last order: "No matter what happens, keep Tomas in sight. Your job is to grab him and run. Don't let anything deter you from that."

His warning had seemed unnecessary at the time, but she understood better now. She heard something rustle in the tree to her right and she could have sworn she felt something on her leg. She didn't bother to look, though. She kept one eye on Tomas and the other on the far side of the house. Time stretched then, suddenly, like a rubber band on the rebound, it snapped and everything happened at once.

A deafening explosion replaced the salsa music that had been playing and screams overtook the sound of laughter. Smoke and another series of smaller explosions came from the far side of the house as the second flash-bang device Cruz had set detonated. Within seconds, a small fire spread across the grass, the chemically fed blaze sending out tendrils in a dozen different directions. People scattered and that's when Julia went into action. The teenagers who'd been guarding the children ran in three separate directions, throwing their drinks to the ground and screaming. Her eyes on Tomas, Julia dashed into the fray and grabbed for him.

She missed.

A woman, running between Julia and the little boy, pushed Julia away as she charged blindly toward her own child. Julia hit the ground hard and cried out instinctively. Swooping a little girl into her arms, the screaming woman carried the child away and never looked back. Scrambling to her feet with a curse, Julia looked around frantically for Tomas.

But he was gone.

Panic surged through Julia with the force of a speeding train. Running against the crowd of people who were trying to escape the spreading flames, she yelled his name. Cruz had warned her there would be tear gas, but the acrid fumes didn't stop her frantic calls. She plowed directly into the cloud, her eyes watering so badly she was blinded, her body racked with deep coughing. She gulped for air and got gas instead, her stomach instantly rebelling.

A second later, in the spreading smoke, a hand grabbed her arm.

Julia wrenched herself free and screamed, lashing out instinctively with her foot to hit her target. She tried to take off again, but the hand came back instantly, and this time the grip was stronger. She whirled sideways and aimed higher. When she kicked this time, though, her foot was captured. She tumbled to the ground and landed with a thud. Cruz's face appeared right in front of her.

"I have him!" Cruz screamed. "I've got Tomas! Let's get the hell out of here!"

CRUZ BLINKED and they were back at the truck. At least, that's how it seemed.

Gripping Julia's hand and carrying Tomas in his arms, they'd vanished into the forest, leaving the fire and wildness behind. Following the same trail they'd taken forty-eight hours before, they'd walked for hours after that, but none of them registered with Cruz. He'd been too busy concentrating on the little boy he carried, the woman beside him and the jungle around them. The last leg of any operation was always the most dangerous. Everyone was exhausted, whether the mission had been successful or not, and the most seasoned of veterans had been known to let down their guard.

Not Cruz.

Even after he pulled the truck into the alley behind Portia's, he stayed alert. He studied the street, then slipped through the garden gate to secure the patio and empty house. The maid was gone, just as Portia had said she would be, and the guard was asleep. A quick tap on the head and he was out. Dragging the man into the garage, Cruz tied his legs and hands and taped his mouth. He wouldn't wake up until they were long gone but if he did, he wasn't going anywhere.

Julia waited for Cruz's sign, then she followed, Tomas in her arms. Only after the three of them were safely inside did Cruz allow himself a sigh of relief.

He carried Tomas up the stairs then left Julia alone with her son. She needed time to reassure herself he was okay, but just as importantly, Cruz needed privacy, too.

TOMAS HAD FALLEN ASLEEP once they'd reached the truck, but the minute Julia put him down on Portia's guest bed, his eyes popped open, just as they always did when it was time for bed. Julia couldn't help herself—she laughed out loud then started to cry. The little boy frowned at his mother's antics but she wrapped her arms around him and murmured her reassurances. A second later he was smiling sleepily.

"I'm so happy to see you, Tomasito." She rained kisses over his face and down his neck. "Did you miss me as much as I missed you?"

He nodded solemnly. "Miss you, Mama," he repeated. "Mama, miss you…"

He patted her face as if to make sure she was real. She captured his fingers and pretended to bite them, a game they'd played since he was a baby. He giggled in response then acted as if he were going to bite her back. A jumble of questions followed, some making sense, some not. She responded in kind, each expression of his more precious to her than ever before. After a few minutes, he grew quiet and asked the question she'd been dreading. "Papa here?"

She swallowed hard. "Papa's not here right now, Tomas," she managed to say. "He's bye-bye."

He accepted her answer with the faith of all children, then his eyelids became heavy again. "Papa gone bye-bye," he echoed. "Papa gone. Mama here…"

He went to sleep immediately and, from the look of him, she knew he'd be out for hours. She couldn't leave him, though. She cuddled him against her, his little-boy smell making her heart swell with relief and fierce love.

She had her child back and no one would ever take him away from her again, she vowed.

No one would take him.

Ever. Again.

WALKING OUTSIDE to the arbor, Cruz pulled out his cell phone and dialed Meredith's number. She answered and he greeted her in Urdu. She responded in kind. The phone was encrypted but not as securely as the one he'd used in the park.

"We got the package," he said. "And everything's okay."

"Did the pickup go smoothly?"

"After a sort," he answered. "You didn't by any chance help me out by making someone disappear, did you?"

"No," she replied. "I didn't, but I know what you're talking about. One of his hired hands got in some trouble in Panama City and he had to go take care of it. He's supposed to be back tomorrow night. She went with him."

"I knew he was gone. When he gets the latest news, he'll be back."

"I'm sure you're right. But you have a few hours at least." She paused. "Are you ready for the party? Is everything in place?"

She meant Miguel's death. Party was a euphemism they'd used for years, but the term suddenly grated on Cruz's sensibilities and he didn't know why.

"We're getting there," he said. "It'll be okay."

"Well, I don't know what your timetable is," she said, "but you need to know his number two is on his way out of town. He's going to visit the resort you just left. He got a frantic call from there about an hour ago, details weren't given. He decided to check out the situation before he called the boss."

"That's good to know," Cruz answered. With Guillermo gone and Miguel frantic over Tomas's disappearance, the final step of this ordeal might be reached sooner than Cruz had thought possible. Security wouldn't be what it normally was because everyone would be looking for the boy. Which meant he might be able to get Julia out of the country ahead of schedule. Things were working out especially well, in more than one arena.

He wouldn't be tempted to do what he shouldn't if Julia were thousands of miles away.

"That's really good," he repeated.

A small silence rolled down the line and Cruz cursed himself. Meredith was a sponge—she absorbed anything and everything that came her way. No nuance was too small for her attention. Her voice held an unfamiliar note when she spoke. "Is everything okay with you two?"

She couldn't speak Julia's name but he understood. "She's fine," he said brusquely. "And so am I."

She confirmed his suspicions with her next question. "Are you fine individually or are you fine, as in 'together'?"

"I don't know what you're asking me," he said without inflection, "but we're fine. Fine as in okay-and-don't-ask-any-more-stupid-questions-dammit."

"All right, all right…" He could imagine her holding up her hands. "It's just that she is my friend and—"

"I know that—"

"And I don't want her hurt—"

"I know that, too." He closed his eyes then reopened them. "She won't be."

"I'm counting on that." Her voice held no more emotion than his, but Cruz heard her warning all the same. They said goodbye and Cruz went back inside Portia's villa.

He was about to open his second beer when Julia came down the stairs a short time later. As she approached, he could see that she'd washed her face and piled her hair on top of her head. A wicked-looking scratch marred her jaw, and a jagged rip ran down one sleeve of her T-shirt. There was a matching one on the opposite leg of her pants. Despite her appearance, she seemed to glow in the dim light that was slipping through the shutters.

"How is he?" Cruz asked unnecessarily.

"He's wonderful." Her smile was wide. "A little confused about everything that happened, but okay other than that. He's already asleep again and by the way he's snoring, I'd say he's going to stay that way for hours."

"We don't have that long. Miguel obviously wasn't at Amalia's, but you can bet someone's tracking him down right now to tell him what happened. As soon as he finds out Tomas is missing, he's going to look for you."

"I've taken care of that. Miguel thinks I'm with Portia. If he calls her looking for me, she'll phone here. We have some breathing room."

Crossing the room to the bar near the couch, she opened one of the bottles of water that lined the shelves. When she put it down, the container was empty. Opening another, she drank it too. Cruz couldn't take his eyes off her.

She came to where he stood and he wondered how she managed to still take away his breath after forty-eight hours in the jungle. They were both filthy, exhausted and raw with nerves, but all he could think about was how her lips had tasted when they'd kissed the day before.

She put her hand on his arm. Two of her already short nails had been broken off, all the way to the quick. He remembered the way he'd labeled her and wondered now how he could have thought that about her.

"I couldn't have done this without you, Cruz. When I lost sight of Tomas in all the confusion—" she shook her head "—I lost it. It was panic city. If you hadn't grabbed him and then found me—"

"You would have pulled yourself together. And done just fine."

"No," she said firmly. "I wouldn't have. I'm stronger than I was last time I tried to escape but I wouldn't have won this one."

"Disagree all you want," he countered, "but when you finish, go get the first-aid kit for me." With a wince, he pulled up his T-shirt to show her the bruise on his chest. It was already turning colors. "I think you might have broken one of my ribs with that first kick."

She gasped, her attention diverted, just as he'd known it would be. "Oh, my God, Cruz. I'm sorry! I didn't know—"

"It's okay," he said. "You did exactly what you should have done. You didn't know it was me."

Making sympathetic sounds, she took his hand and led him upstairs to a bedroom across the hall from where he'd laid Tomas.

"Clean up in there," she said, nodding toward the adjoining bath. "When you finish, come back out and I'll tape your ribs." Closing the door behind her, she left him alone.

When she returned thirty minutes later, she'd bathed, too. Her hair hung around her face like strands of wet gold and she was naked beneath a thin blue robe. Sitting on the bed, Cruz let his eyes linger longer than they should have on the curves beneath the silk. Finally he raised his gaze.

She read the desire that he couldn't hide but she ignored it. Crossing the room, she came to where he sat. With its high bolsters and four posts, the bed was obviously an English antique, at odds with its location but more than suited to its British owner. The thick mattress put him at the perfect height for Julia's ministrations. She put herself between his knees and leaned closer.

Her hands were warm and gentle as they probed his chest and back. "I don't think anything's really broken," she said, stepping back after a minute, "but I hit you pretty hard. Taping those lower ribs would probably still be a good idea."

She unwound the elastic bandage she'd brought with her then rewrapped it around his chest, pulling it tight and tying it off with a twist. When she finished, she didn't move.

"I owe you a debt I can never repay."

"You're going to pay me back," he cautioned. "With interest. Let's leave it at that."

She cradled his jaw with her palms. "I don't want to 'leave it at that.'"

Not knowing what to say, Cruz turned his head until his lips were centered on the palm of her right hand. He kissed it then faced her again. "Julia—"

"I'm not confused now, Cruz." She spoke softly but with force. "And I'm not upset. I have my child and both of us are still alive. I want to be with you."

"No, you don't," he said. "Go away, Julia. Turn around and walk out of here and don't do what you think you want to do. You'll regret it."

Her hands slipped from his face and for a pulse-stopping moment, he thought she was taking his advice.

Instead she dropped her arms to his neck and moved closer.

"I've done plenty of things I regret, Cruz, but I can promise that making love with you isn't going to join that list."

"Because we aren't going to."

She shook her head. "Because I'm not going to regret it."

She pressed her lips to his then pushed him down to the bed.

If Cruz had been a better man, he would have refused Julia's advances, but he was who he was. Shoving Meredith's warning to the back of his mind, he pulled Julia to him and returned her kiss, as he eased back against the pillows. Her lips opened and at that point he knew he was lost.

The silk robe was a fragile barrier but a barrier nonetheless, and he tugged it up, eager to feel her skin instead. A second later he was rewarded, the warmth of her smooth buttocks filling his palms. She moaned into his mouth as he gently squeezed her.

The towel he'd wrapped around his hips came undone and he felt the smooth glide of her legs against his own. Dragging his mouth away from her lips, Cruz kissed her chin and then her neck. Everywhere he touched, with his hands or with his mouth, she was sweet, incredibly sweet. He groaned and let his kisses drop lower. Abandoning her hips, his hands found her breasts, their velvety warmth fueling his desire.

Mindful of her history, Cruz forced himself to slow down. The last thing he wanted to do was make her think she wasn't in control. Taking his lips from her breasts he slid down her body. Stretched above him, she gripped the headboard and groaned deeply in her throat, arching her back to meet his tongue. He continued until she begged him to stop.

Cruz propped himself on his elbows to watch her. Her lips swelling, her wet hair curling, she returned his gaze with a directness that was almost painful. He knew that he'd never seen anything more beautiful and he never would again. Julia was an incredible woman, inside and out.

So what in the hell was she doing with him?

He gave her one last chance to stop them. Pulling back, he looked into her eyes. Their color had changed once more, the bright blue deepening to the shade of a Thai sapphire. "There's no stopping after this," he warned.

"There was no stopping before this," she replied.

JULIA WAS vaguely aware of Cruz slipping on a condom, but where it came from or how he got it, she had no idea. Nor did she care.

Something inside her had changed when Cruz

had appeared out of the smoke and she'd seen her son in his arms. The sight had taken the desire she'd felt for him and made it into a feeling much more powerful. She couldn't call the reaction love; she didn't know him well enough to label it that. But it *was* more than desire. They'd shared a life-changing experience and no matter what happened after this, they were bound by what they'd gone through.

She didn't fully understand, but she knew that her body had led her to this point and she had to follow it. If she didn't, her heart would never be the same.

And Miguel would win, whether he lived or died.

Sensing her determination, Cruz drew her to him with an undeniable insistence and all her thoughts fled. She focused instead on the details of his body—the solid weight of him, the dark curls on his chest, the tapered hips that were now poised over her own.

He kissed her again, his tongue coming into her mouth at the same time he entered her body. As if he were afraid he might scare her, he seemed to hold back, but Julia had been ready for him since she'd walked into his embrace in the jungle. She gripped his arms and lifted herself to meet him, each push bringing with it an exquisite fulfillment.

He increased his rhythm, and she met him thrust for thrust. In the end, they cried out together.

Sated, exhausted and completely wrung out, Julia fell asleep, wrapped in Cruz's embrace.

He lay beside her and waited.

CHAPTER THIRTEEN

TOUCHING HER GENTLY on the shoulder, Cruz woke Julia up an hour later. Her eyes fluttered then she was awake, completely and instantly.

"It's time to get up," he said.

She nodded but, instead of leaving the bed, she reached for him. They kissed and Cruz felt himself falling down a long dark hole. Their caresses turned more heated and before he could stop them, they were making love again. Every time he touched her, he bound himself closer to her. When the time came to sever their connection, the pain was going to stay with him a very long time. Even as he entered her the second time, Cruz knew what he was doing was wrong, but the thought was quickly gone and he kept going.

When they finished, he stared at the ceiling then he kissed Julia one last time and swung his legs over the side of the mattress. He turned to look at her. A stripe of morning sun had fallen across the bed. Lying in the tangled bedding, her blond hair spread over the pillow, her eyes glazed with desire, Julia took away his breath. Just as she had his good sense.

"We need to talk," he said.

She pulled the sheet to her breasts and looked at him, her expression sharpening.

"I found out where Miguel is. He's going to be back sometime today."

"How did you…"

He shook his head and her question faltered.

"You know this for a certainty," she asked instead.

"Yes, I do."

She moved to the edge of the bed, keeping her back to him. Her voice was small. "Then it's tonight?"

A silence that was heavy with expectations built between them. Cruz wasn't sure if they were his or hers. Probably both. "I'm not sure yet."

And he wasn't.

When he'd left Bogota two weeks before, Cruz had had a plan, but things had changed. He had changed. Julia had changed. The whole damn situation had changed. The same kind of doubts that he'd experienced last night when he'd seen the unexpected party hit him again. Having second thoughts was foreign to Cruz and in the past twenty-four hours he'd experienced them twice now. What was going on? What was happening to him? He didn't know, but he had to stop and refocus or disaster was going to follow.

"I'm not sure," he repeated.

She twisted around to look at him, her eyes wide.

"I thought you had it all figured out. I thought as soon as we got Tomas, Miguel would be—"

"I did think that," he answered. "But we have the time. As long as he believes Tomas has been kidnapped, Miguel will be off balance. He'll stay nervous and twitchy until that's resolved."

"What do I do in the meantime?"

"Until you hear from me, nothing." He grabbed his pants off the floor and thrust his legs into them, standing when he finished. "I'll go get Portia at the airport and explain everything. She can take you back to your villa. When Miguel arrives, you play the upset mother like we talked about. Once Miguel is inside the compound, I'll decide where we go from there." He zipped up his pants and reached for his shirt. "Unlock the south gate of the courtyard then sit tight. I'll find you and we'll talk."

"Cruz, is something wrong?" Her voice was tentative, her expression baffled. "I wasn't looking forward to helping you, but I made you a promise and my word is good. I don't understand why you're changing the plan now. Is it because I screwed up with Tomas—"

Angry at himself and the gut-loosening thoughts that were rattling him, Cruz spoke harshly. "I'm changing the plan because I need to, Julia. If you have a problem with that, I'm sorry, but I'm not going to kill Miguel tonight just because you're ready."

She pulled back at the brusqueness in his tone,

and he could see her retreat behind a wall of protective distance. Julia was accustomed to men like him and she knew when to back off. Her reaction made him feel like the bastard he was and once again Cruz was forced to acknowledge the truth—a very thin line separated him and Miguel Ramirez. They were both brutal, self-centered men who focused on a goal and never felt doubt. Even death didn't scare them.

Cruz forced himself to ignore Julia's reaction and his self-admitted flaw.

"I'm going to pick up Portia." He stepped away from the bed. "Be ready to leave when we get back."

DRESSING QUICKLY after Cruz left, Julia walked down the hall to the bedroom where she'd put Tomas. Sitting on the bed and watching him sleep, she wished she had magical powers. She would have stopped the grandfather clock in the hallway from ticking, and at least for a little while, let them exist in a vacuum, safe from the outside world and far away from the terrible things they had facing them.

Not the least of which was her promise to Cruz.

Her payback for his help had been weighing on her mind ever since she'd committed herself to it. Murder was an awful thing, yet the choice was between her son and a man who'd done nothing but try to destroy her. If she'd been the only one affected, her decision might have been different, but she had to protect Tomas.

Cruz's sharp words had left her feeling uneasy and bewildered. What was going on? Why was he suddenly acting as if he didn't trust her? He'd said it didn't matter, but maybe her mistake had bothered him. She'd assumed that making love would bring them closer—it had for her—but it seemed as if just the opposite had happened.

She'd never met a man so complicated and this morning when she'd looked into his eyes, she'd understood something that had escaped her before now. There would always be parts of Cruz that remained behind a locked door. She would never know him completely.

Julia stood up and Tomas grunted in his sleep and rolled over. For reasons she didn't understand, Cruz had stepped behind one of those doors this morning and all she could do was hope he'd come back out. No matter what happened, she decided, she didn't regret what they'd done. The memory of their lovemaking would stay with her forever, even if the man himself didn't.

Cruz and Portia returned an hour later. By the expression on Portia's face when she walked into her living room, Julia knew she would do her part to get Julia and Tomas out of Colombia. The two women embraced tightly then Portia stepped back and held her by the shoulders.

"Why didn't you tell me what you were going to do?" she asked. "I could have done something to help."

"You did help," Julia said. "You just didn't know it."

Portia dropped her hands and unwrapped the shawl from around her shoulders. "You didn't trust me," she said bluntly.

Julia didn't know what to say, but Portia didn't seem to need an answer. "It's all right," she said, reading Julia's reaction. "You did the right thing, sweetheart. When it comes to our children, we all do what we must. Is Tomasito okay? Where is he?"

Relieved, Julia smiled. "He's fine, but very tired. I put him in his favorite room upstairs."

"Good," the older woman said with satisfaction. "Very good. Chita's coming back tonight. I'll have her tend to Jose's headache—" she sent Cruz a wry look that said he'd explained about her guard, too "—and then I'll have her make some soup for dinner. After that, Tomas will go somewhere else."

"But, Portia—"

Cruz interrupted. "It's the only way, Julia. When he runs out of enemies, Miguel will eventually start to search in San Isidro. Portia's name will be on the list."

Portia took Julia's hands in hers. "He'll be safe where I take him. I promise you, sweetheart."

A catch developed in her throat. Julia knew they were right, but the thought of not knowing where Tomas would be was almost more than she could handle.

Portia squeezed her fingers. "I'll guard him with my very life."

"I know you will," Julia answered, and suddenly she did. The anxiety she'd thought she'd sensed in Portia last week had obviously been a reflection of her own nervousness. She met her friend's eyes, the self-confidence Miguel had all but destroyed starting to assert itself once again. "I trust you, Portia."

Julia shifted her gaze and caught Cruz's eyes over the older woman's shoulder. He looked away first.

CRUZ'S ANXIETY CONTINUED to grow, but he ignored it until Portia and Julia headed to the front door to leave for Ramirez's compound. At that point, he drew Julia to one side while Portia continued to the car.

Julia was wary as she looked up at him.

"I'll be there tonight," he said brusquely. "Don't forget about the gate."

They were standing in the shadow of Portia's doorway. Julia's expression shifted at his words. "Do you really think I'd forget?"

"No," he conceded. "I don't but…"

"But what?"

He narrowed his eyes and glanced over her shoulder.

"Cruz?"

The way she said his name made him want to pull her into his arms, slam the door behind them and never open it again. He spoke before he could stop himself. "I just want you to be careful, that's all. Miguel's unpredictable. Watch him closely."

She seemed to consider his warning, then she laid her hand against his jaw with such sweetness that his throat stung.

"It'll be okay," she whispered. "I have all the faith in the world in you, Cruz. You're the only one who could make this happen and I trust you with my life."

I'm not the man you want me to be, he thought, *and I can never become him, either. Even if I wanted to change, I couldn't. I'm Miguel in a different pair of shoes, don't you see that?*

"I don't deserve that kind of confidence," was all he said.

"Then we're going to have to disagree again. You not only deserve it, you've already earned it."

Giving in to the strain that was building inside him, Cruz brought her to him and pressed his mouth against hers, his hands tight on her shoulders. He held the kiss for longer than he should have, but even when it was done, he couldn't let her go. Enveloping her in a hug, he ran his hands over her back and memorized the feel of her body.

Palms on his chest, Julia was the one who separated them. "I'll see you tonight," she said.

He nodded because he couldn't speak. She turned and was gone a moment later.

PORTIA DROPPED Julia off in front of the compound, her bag in hand. Leaning through the open window of the car, Julia spoke softly, her heart aching. "Take care of my baby. I—I almost couldn't leave him."

"I know," Portia answered. "But he'll be fine and this will all be over soon and the two of you can have a normal life. I promise I'll protect him and Cruz will do the same. You can trust him, Julia."

"He's a good man, Portia," she said thickly. "I owe him everything."

"All he wants is your love," the older woman replied. "He's sick with it, you know."

Julia took in a sharp breath. "You're wrong about that."

"I've been wrong about a lot of things in my seventy years," Portia answered, "but this isn't one of them. I can recognize love when I see it."

Julia let the idea roll around in her mind like a loose marble. Love? Was Cruz capable of love? Was love what she even wanted? She'd told him she didn't think that emotion existed, but he'd argued with her. Now here was Portia insisting that was exactly what Cruz felt for Julia. The contradiction bothered her, especially considering what was ahead of them.

She shook her head again then kissed Portia goodbye. As the little red car disappeared around the bend, she picked up her bag and headed inside. Tonight, the only thing she needed to worry about was getting Cruz safely into the compound. He'd decide the best way to proceed from there.

She went directly to her suite and dropped off her overnight bag. The SUV was gone, she noticed, so that mean Guillermo was, too. Going to the kitchen, she prepared herself a *cafe con leche* then she took the mug and walked outside. Strolling from bougainvillea to plumeria, she made her way around the perimeter of the courtyard examining the flowers, occasionally plucking a withered blossom, sometimes stopping to sniff one. She took her time and when she finally made it to the gate and she was sure no one was watching, she turned to face the fountain and leaned against the black wrought iron as if resting. Slipping her right hand behind her, she dropped the latch without a sound. The deed was done and a full second hadn't even passed.

After that, the day passed by slowly, the shadows growing longer and longer until it was finally time for dinner. She picked at a light meal, her nerves too raw and on edge to actually eat, then she settled down to wait in the living room, the book she'd pulled out to distract her lying open but unread on her lap. Who would come first. Cruz or Miguel?

She dozed after a bit then something woke her. Tensing, she listened and the sound she'd come to dread echoed down the tiled hall.

Miguel had arrived. His footsteps were rapid and loud. She interpreted the sound, her heart pounding before he even appeared. He was upset and very angry. He'd heard about Tomas. She told herself this was what she wanted—was what she and Cruz had planned for—but she'd lived too long with the consequences of Miguel's moods not to be shaken. Whatever happened next, it was going to be bad.

He didn't disappoint her. Bursting into the living room, he charged to where she sat, her eyes closed tightly.

"Wake up," he screamed. "Wake up, Julia! Something terrible has happened."

He spoke in Spanish and she cringed inwardly. He'd only done that once before and that had been when she'd tried to escape and failed.

"Wh-what?" She blinked her eyes open as if the light and noise were unexpected. "What's wrong?"

Before he could answer, a throng of men came in through the front door, Guillermo leading them. Julia sat up and suddenly she didn't have to act. Her fear was genuine. The room filled with people, some carrying computers, some talking on cell phones, some merely standing by with automatic weapons cradled in their arms.

"What is it?" She looked at Miguel with alarm. "What's going on?"

When he didn't answer, she repeated his name. "Miguel?"

The room fell silent and she let her eyes scan the

crowd until she came to Guillermo. Her gaze lingered on his face and he looked away first. She turned back to the man she'd thought was her husband.

"What's wrong?" she asked again.

Some nameless emotion flashed in his eyes. If he'd been someone else, she might have called it madness, but she knew better. It was evil.

"Tomas is gone."

She blinked and tried to imagine how she'd react if she didn't know the truth. "Gone? What are you talking about? I thought he was with you."

"He was. But something happened and he was taken. We don't know who has him, but we're trying to figure it out." He paused. "When we do, I will hunt them down and crush them. They'll beg for their own deaths."

He spoke calmly, but there was craziness in his eyes and a cold chill rippled down her spine. Just as she'd told Cruz, Miguel didn't doubt her. He was so upset he hadn't even noticed the scratches she'd tried to hide with makeup. He didn't know who to suspect. Despite that, his words gave her the impetus she'd needed.

"What do you mean, he's been 'taken'?" she cried. "What happened? Where is he? What have you done with my baby?" She jumped up and ran toward Miguel, but Guillermo stepped between them.

"What have you done, Miguel?" She struggled

against the bodyguard's grip. "What did you do? What kind of trick is this?"

"It's not a trick." He jerked his head at Guillermo and the man released her. She rubbed her arms and stared at Miguel. "There was an attack on the villa where we were staying. In the confusion, he was grabbed. They got away with him before my people knew what was going on."

At the back of the room, a cell phone rang and the men resumed their tasks, setting up their computers and various equipment, their muttered conversations starting over.

"When did this happen?" She forced herself to step closer. "Tell me everything!"

He gave her the briefest of details. Had the situation been genuine, she would have been beside herself. Realizing that, she pushed him for more, but he gave her nothing else.

"At least, tell me what are you going to do," she begged. "I have to know—"

"I'm not *going* to do anything," he interrupted. "I'm already doing it. In the meantime, I want you in your room. Stay there and don't come out. I don't need your hysterics adding to the problem."

"He's my son, too," she cried. "Don't make me stay there, Miguel. I need to know what's happening—"

"I'll tell you everything I think you need to know," he said in a dismissive voice. Catching Guillermo's eyes, he jerked his head. "Take her to her room," he said, "and lock the door."

"Miguel! Please! Don't do this!" She continued to plead even as Guillermo took her arm. "You're not being fair—"

Tugging her out of the room, Guillermo shook his head in warning. "Forget it," he muttered. "He isn't going to listen to you. He's not listening to anyone. He's gone *loco...*"

She yanked her arm from the bodyguard's grip. "Tell me what you know," she pleaded. "Please, Guillermo!"

"There was an explosion," he said, "and a fire. Nothing major, no one hurt. Afterward, they realized it was all a diversion. One of the women thinks she saw a *gringo* but she wasn't sure. She couldn't give any kind of description except to say the guy was skinny and Anglo and he was trying to grab Tomas. He disappeared before she could get help."

Julia began to cry, the tears coming easily since she was so on edge. A second later, they reached her room. She turned as Guillermo stood in the doorway.

"Please don't lock it," she begged. "I won't tell him."

He gave her a stony look, then he stepped out and closed the door. The bolt clicked behind him.

CHAPTER FOURTEEN

LYING IN THE GRASS above the Ramirez villa, Cruz adjusted his binoculars and watched Guillermo walk away from Julia's suite. He'd only caught a glimpse as they'd left the main house and headed toward the southern section of the compound, but it was all Cruz had needed. His heart felt as if it were about to explode and anger took over from the cool, dispassionate attitude that normally served him.

He should never have asked Julia to help him.

It'd been a bad idea from the very beginning and once they'd made love, it had become even worse. What in the hell had he been thinking?

He dropped his glasses and closed his eyes, refusing to soften his self-recrimination. She was a normal person, for God's sake. An ordinary woman who ought to be living in suburbia, planning dinner parties and worrying about her hips. She wasn't a killer. He'd been wrong, wrong, wrong to demand that she help him.

And he'd been even more wrong to make love with her. They didn't have any kind of future together. His only job was to get her and her son the hell out of Colombia and then he had to get himself the hell out of her life. What had he been thinking? Once Julia Vandamme cleared the border of Colombia, she'd want nothing reminding her of the violence she'd experienced, and that included Cruz.

He grabbed his backpack, stuffed his binoculars into the side pocket, then stood, a clear sense of purpose in mind. Heading down the slope, he felt good for the first time in days.

He knew what he had to do.

An hour later he was inside the compound. Just as he'd predicted, Miguel's security had all but disappeared. He had every available man working to find his son. Still, hugging the wall of the courtyard, Cruz moved through the darkness like a shadow. He couldn't take his good luck for granted.

He made his way to Julia's suite first, cursing under his breath. If he'd bugged her room as he'd planned to the last time he'd been there, he'd have a better idea of what was going on now, but he'd run out of time. He should have let her do the job, but he hadn't trusted her to do it right. Now he was flying blind. Her shadow moved behind the curtains, but her door was bolted shut. He hesitated for a moment and pondered the meaning of this new development. Why had Ramirez had this done? What was going on that he didn't want Julia to know about? Cruz reached for the lock, then stopped. She was probably safer where she was. He'd see what was going on and then return.

He eased around the exterior, pausing to look through the living-room windows. Before he'd come down the hill, he'd seen most of the men leave, but a few were still packing up. Jorge Guillermo was directing their activities. There was no sign of Ramirez.

The development had puzzled Cruz, but he knew Tomas was still safe and that was all he really cared about. They hadn't found the child. He watched the activity a bit longer, though, and a new detail emerged.

Guillermo was acting with an authority Cruz hadn't seen before and the men who were following his orders did so with alacrity. Their movements were quick and nervous, one eye on their task, one eye on Guillermo.

Cruz had been studying Ramirez's setup for months, and he knew the dynamics behind the man's organization. There was only one thing that could have put Jorge Guillermo in charge.

Surprised but not really, Cruz moved away from the window and continued his progress. Power could shift rapidly within the circle of violence that made up the world where Julia's husband lived. Regardless of that fact, Cruz still had to make sure they'd changed the way *he* wanted them to.

He made his way to Ramirez's suite and tested the door. It wasn't locked and again, he wasn't surprised.

Slipping inside the bedroom, he let his eyes adjust to the empty darkness. Navigating past the ornate but primitive furniture, Cruz walked stealthily to Miguel Ramirez's bathroom. As in Julia's suite, no expense had been spared. The white marble gleamed and the gold fixtures glittered. Luxurious thick towels were piled by the whirlpool bath. Light from an elegant chandelier illuminated it all.

Unfortunately, what was lying on the floor wasn't elegant or graceful. Cruz took it all in. He heard the noise behind him a second too late.

Pain exploded behind his right ear. With a gasp, he went down on one knee. Gripping the edge of his consciousness with fierce determination, Cruz struggled to stay focused, but the floor was wet. He lost his balance and went down hard, another blow landing on the back of his head as he fell.

His cheek hit the marble with a thud, the sick odor of splattered blood reaching him. The last thing he saw was a pair of black heels and trim ankles. In complete disbelief, he thought of Julia then everything went black.

JULIA WAITED for Cruz until two, then she fell asleep. Her nightmares were so real that when she woke up a few hours later, she felt even more exhausted than she had before. Fighting smoke and battling blindness, she'd looked for Tomas in her dreams, but her search had taken place in slow motion and instead

of Cruz appearing with her son, Miguel had materialized out of the confusion.

Holding Tomas, he'd laughed at her then vanished.

She woke up with Tomas's name on her lips.

Shaking her head, Julia unfolded herself from the
chair and walked into her bathroom. She splashed
her face with cold water, but it did nothing to help
her red eyes. She wondered briefly if she might have
missed Cruz. If he'd tried the door and found it
locked, would he persist or simply turn around and
leave? She answered herself before the question was
even complete—he would have found a way inside.

She left the bathroom and crossed to the door.
Wrapping her hand around the knob, she turned it as
gently as possible.

The door swung inward without a sound.

She sucked in a shocked breath, her pulse leap-
ing as she peered through the threshold and gazed out
to the courtyard. There wasn't a person in sight. Even
the wind was still. Expecting someone to stop her,
she took a step out then stopped.

Something didn't feel right.

Licking her lips, Julia turned to her right and
started down the open walkway that led to the main
part of the house. Pulling back the heavy door, she
entered. None of the noises she expected—the clat-
ter of conversation and machines, the sounds of cell
phones and faxes—were audible. The house wasn't

just quiet, it was deadly quiet. Swallowing a knot of fear, she forced herself forward.

The living room was deserted, but the men had left their mark. The tabletops were littered with glasses and ashtrays, and a dozen plates, smeared with the remnants of *tortas* and *empanadas,* were scattered about. The brass trash can, a decorative more than functional item, overflowed with crumpled papers. They'd been gone a while; the cigarette smoke was stale and the ice had melted in their drinks.

Where was everyone?

Where was Miguel?

Julia couldn't recall a time when she'd been completely alone inside the house. From the day she'd moved in, there had been servants and cooks and guards about. Even if everything had been all right, the eerie quiet would have been uncomfortable, but contrasting the situation now to the craziness of a few hours before, Julia felt her unease grow exponentially.

She called out, her voice sounding tentative. "Hello? Is anyone here? Hello?"

No one answered.

She headed for the kitchen but it was deserted, too. She passed through several other areas and came out of the main building on the opposite side of the courtyard. She didn't visit this part of the compound very often. It was Miguel's and she tried to avoid it.

There was no way to get around it now, though. She had to figure out what was going on and that meant finding Miguel.

Taking a deep breath, she let it out slowly before knocking on the door of his *casita*. The sound seemed empty to her. When he didn't answer, she tried the doorknob and the door opened unexpectedly, swinging gently back as though it were inviting her in. It hadn't even been latched. The lapse in security was astonishing. Miguel never let details like that slide.

"Miguel? Are you in there?"

Daylight had yet to break and there were deep shadows in every corner. Heavy furniture, crudely made with rough edges and uneven lines, filled the room. He'd explained when she'd first seen it—"The locals make it," he'd said. "And I keep it to remind myself of who I really am."

Entering the suite, she called out again. "Miguel? It's Julia. What's going on?"

The silence seemed even louder here than it had in the living room. She took another two steps inside. The coverlet on the bed was smooth and unwrinkled. Wherever Miguel had gone, he'd left without getting any sleep. There were no clothes strewn around, no discarded shoes, no sign that he'd even been there.

But he *had* been.

Julia could sense his presence. In fact, it was so strong she decided instantly he probably hadn't left at all. He was still there, she told herself in a shaky voice. She could feel him. She could smell him.

She gave the bed wide berth and moved toward the rear of the suite. His rooms were the mirror image of her own, and she needed no light to find her way to the bathroom.

The door was half open.

She called out again. No answer. She took another step. Then she pushed at the door. With her foot.

It didn't move.

Something slithered up her spine.

She spoke his name one last time. "Miguel?"

Even though she'd begun to suspect that she knew what was behind the door, she had to see for herself. She put the palms of her hands against the smooth mahogany and pushed.

Her effort met with resistance. Something behind the door was blocking it. She tried again and it gave slightly so she put her shoulder to the wood and pressed harder. A gap, just wide enough for her to squeeze through, appeared and she wormed her way inside.

She froze, and her brain processed the scene the only way it could. As separate packets of information.

Miguel was on the floor. He was naked. And he was dead.

Cruz had come and killed Miguel.

She gasped and stumbled sideways, hitting the

marble counter with her hip as she nudged Miguel's right foot. His leg been lodged against the door, holding it shut. As Julia moved out of the way, his foot flopped back with a dull thud and the door shut once again.

There was a hole was in his chest, a small, round hole, less than a centimeter in diameter. It didn't seem possible that the amount of blood beneath him—so wide, so red, so shocking—could have been caused by a hole that tiny.

She couldn't take her eyes from the dark pool. Along the edge, the blood was smeared as if someone had stepped in it. A long red ribbon stretched to the doorway, as well. Had there been a struggle afterward? How long had he been dead? Was Cruz nearby?

Questions flooded her mind but then she heard something outside. Thinking it might be Cruz, she turned expectantly.

The door burst open so quickly she had to jump out of the way, the heavy mahogany missing her by inches. Her eyes flew to the man on the threshold, but it wasn't Cruz.

A San Isidro policeman stared back, his gun drawn, his nerves taut. His eyes went to the dead man on the floor then back to her.

Jorge Guillermo stood behind the cop and a woman stood behind Jorge. She was young and beautiful and she looked very much like Catherine Zeta-Jones.

HE CAME TO in solid darkness and for a single second, Cruz couldn't catch his breath. The ache in his head registered, though, and he gasped. The moment before he was hit returned, the throbbing pain bringing it back with a clarity he didn't expect.

He raised himself to his hands and knees then he collapsed again.

Holding back the nausea, he hung his head and concentrated on the rough wooden floor tilting beneath his knees. When the spinning slowed and finally stopped, he pushed a hand to his right. His fingers hit a stuccoed wall. Removing his left boot, he left it at that point, then he continued, his fingers following the roughness until he came to a corner. In what felt like only a second, he found his boot again. He put it back on, then slowly stood, his hands extended beyond his head. When he touched the ceiling, he was still crouching.

The room couldn't have been more than five feet long and four feet wide. And it was a little under six feet high. It had no door.

He repeated his circuit, this time brushing the ceiling with his hand. Halfway down and midway across, he felt the rough outline of a framed opening. The boards that covered it had been nailed together carefully but something else was over them, too. No light could be seen through the cracks his fingernails found.

He wasn't in a room. He was in a pit.

He pressed his hands against the boards. They didn't move. He hadn't expected they would, but this time he felt the heat he'd missed before. The hole was outside and the sun was hitting it. How long had he been there? Was it still the same day or had he been out longer? He rubbed his hand over his jaw and decided hours had probably passed instead of days.

Sitting on the floor, he closed his eyes against the blackness and concentrated. The only thing he could remember seeing was a pair of black high heels. He forced himself to think harder and the blurry image sharpened. A pants leg came into focus and he let his mind follow it. Denim, he thought quietly. The woman had had on denim.

The pain in his head had receded but it came back suddenly, like the wash from a tide. He thought of Julia as she'd gotten into Portia's red car. She'd had on jeans, he remembered. Blue jeans. He opened his eyes, but the image wouldn't go away.

THE POLICEMAN STEPPED over Miguel's body and reached for Julia. She struggled but her efforts were pointless. The handcuffs, old-fashioned metal ones, snapped around her wrists and the fight was over.

All she could think about was the first time she'd talked to Cruz.

If you don't see things my way, I can pretty well guarantee you'll be arrested for Miguel Ramirez's

*murder. He is going to die and you'll be the only one
left for the* policia *to blame.*

Her eyes sought Guillermo's. "I didn't do this,"
she said. She made her voice calm, despite the storm
raging inside her. "I didn't—"

"Don't bother, Julia." He nodded to the woman at
his side. "We knew what you were going to do." He
looked briefly at Miguel's body. "I'm only sorry we
didn't get here sooner."

He was lying. It shone in his eyes. Julia turned to
the cop who held her, but he didn't care and even if
he had, she realized suddenly, it wouldn't have mattered. Guillermo and Amalia Riveria had taken
Miguel's place. Just like that. The policeman wasn't
dumb and he knew which direction to swing his alle-
giance.

Julia tightened her jaw. "I didn't shoot Miguel
and you know it."

"Lo siento, señora." Amalia spoke for the first
time. Her voice was low and melodious. "But you are
wrong. In fact, you've been wrong about a lot of
things." She reached into her pocket and flipped
something to Julia's feet. "And your judge of character is sorely lacking."

Julia's eyes followed the flutter. Amalia had
thrown a package of matches that had a black cover
with a yellow rose adorning the front flap. They
were just like the ones Miguel had found in Julia's
purse. She'd thought Cruz had put them there, but

he'd denied it. Her throat tightened as she met Amalia's eyes.

"He's been working with us all along."

Julia let Amalia's words soak in. She could almost feel their oily presence against her skin. She wanted to be shocked, but she wasn't. Not really. Cruz himself had told her he didn't deserve her confidence. How much clearer could he have been?

Despite her better judgment, a tiny part of her heart argued against the betrayal. "You're lying."

Amalia shook her head, her black hair sliding over her shoulders in a sensual wave. Her expression almost held pity. "Did you really think Guillermo didn't know? The secret meetings, the clandestine plans... The *Americano* is good, but he's not that good." She nodded toward the matches. "That was his signal," she said. "He slipped those in your purse. When Jorge found them, we knew Señor Cruz was on his way to convincing you."

"That's not what happened—"

"You're wasting your breath. I know you wanted him dead. I tried to tell Miguel, but he refused to listen to me. His revenge meant more than anything else. The only way I could prove your intent was to let you try." She shook her head. "I never thought you'd succeed, though."

Her grief was a mockery. She wasn't mourning Miguel's death any more than she was making sense.

Julia stared at her in numbed confusion. "What revenge are you talking about?"

Acting as if she were about to cry, Miguel's mistress ignored Julia's question and abruptly buried her face against Guillermo's chest. He wrapped his arms around her and raised his eyes to Julia's.

She understood instantly, her whole body going cold. Amalia, Guillermo and Cruz had planned everything and, like a puppet, Julia had danced while they'd pulled the strings.

Even Tomas's rescue had probably been part of their plan. Her knees buckled as Julia thought of her son. Was Portia in on it, too? What about Meredith?

Something shattered inside her, the pieces as sharp as jagged glass. Her life was over. She'd lost her son, her chance for freedom, even her heart. She'd risked it all in a trade with the devil and she'd lost.

HE WASN'T SURE how long it took him, but by the time Cruz worked the blade out of the sole of his boot and the handle from the seam in his pants, the sun had moved. The boards overhead were hotter than they had been and he thought he could see a line of light. After this much darkness, the eyes began to play tricks, though, so he couldn't tell for certain.

He pounded the edge into the tang then tested the two pieces to make sure they were secure. The weapon wasn't a hundred percent but at this point, it was better than nothing. He could use it to create confusion, and that was all he needed to regain control.

He sat down and waited for them to come, trying to figure out where he'd gone so wrong.

The night he'd gotten the assignment, after Armando had left, Meredith had returned to Cruz's room. She'd told him about Julia's parents, but had sworn him to secrecy. They were still active, she'd said, although Julia had no idea of their true vocation.

Phillip Vandamme wasn't the bureaucrat his daughter had always thought he was, and her mother had been much more than a secretary. They were high-level communication experts for the U.S. government and years before she'd been born, they'd run the southwestern quadrant of Latin America.

Their protective and restrictive parenting had been a necessary accompaniment to their work. Their one breach in security—which had caused Phillip's so-called accident with the saw—had led them to even tighter watchfulness. Once Julia had left home, however, they'd been unable to control her life. Or her marriage.

They hadn't trusted Miguel Ramirez from the start. He was very clever, though, and Julia had been living in San Isidro for almost two years before they were able to break through his cover story. That's when they learned his father and brother had both died in prison, a place they'd been put thanks to the agents the Vandammes had controlled.

His simple plan had become obvious. Since they'd stolen his family, Miguel Ramirez had decided to steal theirs.

Julia had been his payback. He'd wanted revenge on the Vandammes and he had needed an heir. With her, he'd gotten both.

As soon as they'd understood what was going on, the Vandammes had tried to get the government they served so faithfully to help them, but they'd met with resistance. Finally they'd gone to Meredith. She'd been willing to go it alone, she'd told Cruz, but then she'd learned of Miguel's plans to expand. The risk that posed to the DEA agents who were already in place had been enough to get government cooperation. She'd gotten the sanction and had taken the next flight out, turning the job over to Cruz.

He cursed softly in the darkness.

Only one thing had turned out right in this whole damn mess and that was the fact Miguel Ramirez was dead.

He was dead, but Cruz hadn't had a thing to do with it.

CHAPTER FIFTEEN

THE POLICE STATION in San Isidro consisted of two cells at the back of a dirty office. The city had never needed more. Miguel had run the town. He'd been cop, jury and judge. Most of the offenders he saw were serving their sentences in hell.

She wondered why the police had even been called. Why hadn't Cruz simply taken care of Julia himself? The only reason she could think of was her family—maybe he thought they'd begin to worry about their daughter and would contact the embassy. He wouldn't want that kind of publicity. Clearly he hadn't been aware that her parents hadn't contacted Julia in more than a year. The longer she thought about it the more she understood. His association with Meredith had obviously been a lie as well. Cruz had tricked Julia just as surely as Miguel Ramirez had.

The cop pushed her into one of the cells, then left. Julia sat down on the metal bunk screwed into the wall, grateful for the numbness that had swept over her somewhere between the compound and town. She couldn't let herself think about Tomas or she'd lose her mind. The image of Miguel's body, lying on the floor, came into her mind, but she pushed that away, too.

Instead, she let herself concentrate on one face—Jonathan Cruz's. She thought about him for a very long time. In fact, it was dark outside when she finally stopped thinking about him and everything he had done.

The first thing she would do after she escaped—and she *would* escape—would be to find her son.

The next thing she'd do would be to find Cruz. He was the second man who'd betrayed her—but he would be the last, of that she was sure.

SOMEONE WAS APPROACHING the pit. Cruz heard footsteps above his head and then voices, one low, one higher, filtered down. Two people, he guessed, a man and a woman. They stopped right above him and peeled back the covering that had been over the boards. Light stabbed through the cracks and Cruz stared directly at it, forcing his eyes to adjust. When the trap door jerked open, he tensed.

A ladder was lowered.

"Get out," Jorge Guillermo ordered.

Cruz slipped the shank of his knife into his sleeve and started up the ladder. He had two choices: make a move as soon as he reached the top or bide his time and do it when he was sure of success. When he grabbed the last rung, he paused warily and decided to wait. Guillermo stood to the right of the hole and a woman to the left. She wore blue jeans and black heels. And she wasn't Julia.

Cruz pulled his body up and then out, his eyes sweeping past Guillermo and his companion to orient himself. The hole was inside a fenced square of concertina wire, maybe twelve feet in diameter, with a small stucco shack to one side. His gaze slid past the fence to the walls of the compound, and he remembered Julia's story. This was where Ramirez had kept her the first time she'd tried to escape.

Cruz turned to the woman. She had to be Amalia Riveria, and clearly he'd seen her feet—not Julia's—just before he'd been knocked unconscious. Because he'd seen this story play out too many times to count, the pieces of the puzzle fell into place. Guillermo's attitude. Miguel's body. Amalia's presence. A coup had taken place.

Someone—probably Guillermo, maybe Amalia, possibly both—had decided to take advantage of the confusion, just as he and Julia had planned on doing. With Miguel distracted by Tomas's disappearance, they'd killed him and taken control of his operation. Cruz's chest felt tight. So where was Julia? And what about Tomas? Were they safe? Or were they dead?

Cruz played it cool. "How long have you been planning your little rebellion, Jorge? Was your trick with the matches supposed to help start it?"

The Colombian narrowed his eyes then shrugged. "I wanted to know who you really are, but when I couldn't find out, I remembered you said you were from Texas. I didn't think it'd hurt the situation but Miguel didn't bite…"

"Then you tried to kidnap Julia. But that didn't work out too well, either, did it?"

"You had a lucky break," he said. "We thought her disappearance might distract Miguel but we weren't counting on you. So, tell us, 'Stan MacDuff' who you really are—"

"Who I am is the last thing you need to worry about right now, Jorge. As it is—"

Amalia spoke. "As it is, you are correct. Your presence here doesn't matter now. You've done us a favor by creating such confusion and we're grateful. But you have to tell me where the boy is." She stood quietly, the sun giving her black hair blue highlights. "Until I know where he is, your life, I'm afraid, will not be an easy one."

That answered one question. At least Tomas was still secure.

"It never has been," Cruz said, turning to her. "I doubt seriously whether or not you can make me care."

She smiled. It was a seductive expression, and all at once he understood why she and Miguel had been so evenly matched. She'd used him as much as he'd used her, Cruz decided, manipulating Ramirez with her beauty and controlling him with her body.

"I think you underestimate me," she said. "Surely you didn't think Miguel was the brains behind our operation."

"I never thought about it, Amalia." He let his eyes caress her body. It wasn't a hard task, but once again Cruz was forced to note the similarities between himself and Miguel. Amalia Riveria was exactly the kind of woman Cruz would have had at his own side at one time.

His attention went back to her face where it lingered on her mouth. "Looking at you, I would say anything is possible, but I've been known to be wrong once or twice."

He took a step toward her. Out of the corner of his eye, he saw Guillermo move, too, but Amalia shot the other man a warning look. Guillermo fumed silently but stayed put as Amalia closed the gap between herself and Cruz. The scent of roses came with her.

"You've been wrong about a *lot* of things," she said, looking up at him. "And so has *tu amora*."

"She's not my girlfriend. I'm into brunettes." Staring straight into Amalia's black eyes, Cruz denied Julia without blinking. "Besides that, I don't mix business and pleasure." He smiled at her lazily. "But for you I might make an exception."

She moved another inch closer. Her eyelashes brushed her cheek, then came back up. "I admit I'm intrigued. But first, you must tell me, Señor Cruz,

which was which? You obviously wanted to kill
Miguel and you were using *la rubia* to help you. Was
that business or was that pleasure? If she wasn't your
lover, does that mean she was your employer? She
was very quick to believe you were the one who shot
Miguel."

His stomach turned over, but Cruz made his voice
husky as he reached out and cupped Amalia's jaw.
"Why do you care?"

She didn't move. "Who says I do?"

"Your eyes speak for you," he countered. "They
tell me you still love Miguel and want to find the
blonde so you can see that she suffers as you have."

"You misunderstand." She shook her head
slightly. "I could care less about her. I only want to
know where the boy is. My son is all I care about."

He arched an eyebrow. "*Your* son?"

Her cheeks darkened. "Yes," she said forcefully.
"He is *my* son. If you know where he is, now is the
time to tell me."

"I'd be happy to." Cruz dropped his hand to her
neck as if to caress her and her eyes filled with satisfaction. She thought she'd won. He spoke softly,
"But first—"

Cruz had the knife at her throat before Amalia
could take her next breath. Guillermo reacted fast
and started toward them, but Cruz flipped Amalia
around so her back was against his chest. Dropping
his arm across her windpipe, he tightened his hold.

"But first," he repeated, "you're going to tell me where Julia is."

She didn't answer and Guillermo stepped forward again. With his eyes on the other man, Cruz pressed the tip of his blade to Amalia's neck until a pearl of blood welled. She cried out and Guillermo pulled a small pistol from his pocket.

"Forget it," Cruz said calmly. "She'll be dead before you could even aim, and I don't need the knife to make it happen." He put the weapon into his belt and put the flat of his hand against her neck. "Do you want to risk it?"

Amalia made a gurgling sound. Cruz loosened his hold then shook her. "Tell him."

She spoke hoarsely. "Don't be stupid, Guillermo."

Cruz nodded to the pit. "Drop the gun and get in," he said. "When you're at the bottom, push the ladder back up."

Guillermo didn't move and Amalia screamed at him in Spanish. "Do it, *idioto!* Do what he says!"

With a searing look in Cruz's direction, Guillermo climbed down. A second later, the ladder came back up.

Within his arms, Amalia started to turn and Cruz let her. She looked at him and smiled with a sensual promise. "Tell me where he is," she whispered.

He looked at her through heavy lids. "You first," he whispered.

One corner of her mouth went up. "All right," she

said smugly. "I'll be happy to go first, but you can do nothing about it once you learn the truth."

"I'll be the judge of that."

"She's in jail in San Isidro. Someone informed the police and they arrested her for Miguel's murder. I'm not sure why, but she believes you made that call."

Without thinking, Cruz tightened his embrace, a crushing frustration sweeping through him. He couldn't tell which made him feel worse—the fact that Julia was in a shit hole like the San Isidro jail or the fact that she believed he'd put her there. Either way, Amalia's strategy was clever and he found himself almost admiring her. If she'd killed Julia outright, Amalia would have had nothing left to trade for information. With Julia in jail, though, Amalia not only had a bargaining chip, she also gained the appearance of being a law-abiding citizen, something that would sit well with the authorities should anyone decide to investigate.

"Justice must be served, you know." Amalia's taunting voice pulled him back from this thoughts. "We should all pay for our sins."

"You're right," he said quietly. "When I figure out what you owe, I'll be back to collect."

He picked her up before she could process his words and stepped to the hole where Guillermo waited. He dropped her inside. She was still screaming when he pushed the trapdoor in place.

"DON'T DO ANYTHING rash." Meredith spoke with authority. "I'm in Cartagena. If I catch the next flight out, I can meet the British woman and the child in Panama City, then I'll come there and help—"

"I'm not waiting for you. I'm not waiting for anything! Dammit to hell, Meredith, don't you understand what's happening here? I can't—"

"All right! Okay! Settle down, Cruz. If you don't want to wait for me then at least let me get you some help. I have someone in Cali. He could be there within a few hours and work with you until I arrive. If you go in alone, you'll screw things up."

"She's in jail, Meredith! I'm not gonna sit on my ass and wait for some yahoo to get here when it's convenient. I want her out of there! Now!"

Aiming one of Ramirez's SUVs with one hand, Cruz gripped the phone with his other, plunging down a narrow street at breakneck speed.

After locking the trapdoor, he'd dashed to Portia's to make sure Tomas was all right. She'd made a phone call and, as if by magic, Tomas had appeared. As he'd played on the patio, Cruz had pressed a wad of hundred-dollar bills into Portia's hands and told her what to do. Her little red car had spun out of the driveway five minutes later.

Cruz had taken off in the opposite direction and called Meredith.

"I'm not waiting," Cruz repeated now. "It's too

dangerous. And your man might not be able to leave."

"If he can't, then you'll just have to hang on until I can get there," Meredith replied. "I've gotten more than one or two people out of jail, you know."

"I don't care if you've sprung an army. This is Julia we're talking about, Meredith!"

"I know that, Cruz." Her voice went hard. "You don't have to remind me. I've already got people on the way to take care of Guillermo and Riveria. At the very least, wait for them. They could help you, too, if you'll just sit tight."

"You take care of Tomas," he replied coldly. "I'm going to get Julia."

CRUZ STRODE into the police station with one thing on his mind—Julia. He didn't have a plan, but something would come to him, he was sure. A single cop sat behind the desk, his shoulder immobilized by a white sling. He looked up as the door closed behind Cruz, and their eyes met. The uniformed man turned pale beneath his cap.

"Lieutenant Jimenez." Forcing himself to stay calm when he'd rather be screaming, Cruz stared down at the cop who'd given Cruz the floor plan to Amalia Riveria's villa. "I see you're in charge tonight."

The man nodded.

"Are you alone?"

The cop found his voice. *"Sí, señor."*

"But not completely. You have a prisoner in the back."

"Sí, señor." In a protective gesture, he put his hand on his sling.

"You know who she is?"

"Sí. It's Señora Ramirez."

"Do you know why she's in jail?"

"She killed the *señor.*"

Cruz moved to the man's desk and perched on one edge. The cop flinched at the movement.

"How's the shoulder?" Cruz asked.

"Bueno," he said as beads of sweat formed a line across his upper lip. *"Muy bueno."*

"That's good," Cruz answered. "I bet it hurt a lot at first. Injuries like that usually do."

The cop nodded.

"You wouldn't want anything else like that to happen, would you?"

It took him a moment but Jimenez shook his head. "No. I would not want that to happen."

Cruz leaned closer. "Then open the cell door and let *la señora* out. You take her place." He paused. "Otherwise you're going to have another accident."

For a man with a dislocated shoulder, the lieutenant moved quickly.

Julia walked out of the cell, rubbing her wrists and looking confused until she saw Cruz. Then she stopped abruptly and even took a step back. "What are you doing here?"

Her voice was hostile and her eyes held all the suspicion—and more—that he'd seen in them the first time they'd met.

"I've got the SUV outside," he answered. "Let's go then I'll explain."

She stood her ground. "Where's my son?"

"He's safe. Portia has him. Here, you can call her." He held his cell phone out to her, but she wouldn't take it. "You can ask her where they are. I sent them to the airport and told her to take the next flight out. Meredith's meeting them in Panama City. Portia bought us tickets, and she's leaving them at the counter." He reached into his back pocket and removed Julia's passport. "I took this from Miguel's office, along with Tomasito's. I gave his to Portia," he said. "Call her. She'll tell you," he repeated.

Julia snatched her passport from him. "I'm not calling anyone. If I call, they'll know I'm out." She shook her head almost violently. "I'm on my own now."

Cruz tried to close the distance between them, his hand outstretched, but Julia backed away from him, her eyes as hard as ice.

"I know what you did," she said coldly. "And I'd like to make you a promise—"

"Julia, please—"

"After I have my son back and he's safe, I'll find

you." She continued as if he hadn't spoken. "And when I do, we're going to discuss what you did to me and how you used me. You're going to be sorry, Cruz. Very, very sorry."

"I didn't betray you. I know Amalia and Jorge told you that I set you up, but—"

She interrupted him as he had her, her voice detached. "You know, Cruz, you're really a remarkable man. In the short time we've been together, I've learned almost as much from you as I did from Miguel."

The steel in her voice pierced his heart. Cruz closed his eyes and let the gash bleed.

"One of the most important lessons I learned is that I can trust myself. *And no one else.*"

He opened his eyes and met her gaze.

"So that's exactly what I'm going to do. The rest of you," she said softly, "can go straight to hell. It's where you belong."

THE FIRST TIME Miguel had allowed Julia to visit the market after she'd tried to escape, she'd lied to him and said she'd lost twenty pesos. Ever since that day, she'd kept those folded notes in whichever shoes she had on. Walking out of the police station, she flagged a cab, climbed in and removed her left sneaker to pull out one of the bills. She gave him Portia's address.

It was the last place Julia had seen Tomas, so it would be the first place she would search.

Portia's security guard watched as Julia climbed

out of the cab then strode toward his shack. He flinched and touched the large white bandage at the back of his head.

"*La señora* isn't here," he said, his eyes going wide at Julia's disheveled appearance. "She took off an hour ago, maybe more. Right after the *Americano* came."

Julia's throat tightened. "Did she have my son with her?"

Obviously in quandry, the guard blinked at her question. Julia helped him resolve his dilemma. She stepped up to him, grabbed a handful of his shirt and pulled him to her with one swift yank. "Did—she—have—my—son?"

She didn't know if it was her voice or the look in her eyes that worked. She didn't care.

"*Sí, señora, sí, sí. El niño* was with her, *sí, sí.*"

"Where were they going?"

"I—I don't know," he stuttered, "but she had a bag. The one she takes with her when she goes to Medellin."

Releasing the man, Julia ran in the villa and quickly found what she needed. Ten minutes later she was back out the door.

CRUZ TAPPED his driver on the shoulder and pointed to the cab Julia climbed into. He'd ditched the SUV at the police station and had followed Julia to Portia's in his own cab and now she was leaving once more.

"That's her," he said.

The man grunted and put his car in gear.

"Not too close," Cruz warned.

He got a second grunt in reply. Within moments, Cruz knew Julia was going to the airport to check out his story.

The car sped through the gates that led to the terminal fifteen minutes later.

They pulled up and Cruz thrust a handful of pesos into the front seat as he got out, his eyes on Julia who was climbing out of her cab. She walked directly inside, looking neither right nor left. She moved with the same kind of grace she always had, but there was even more determination in her step than usual.

Throwing some more pesos to a kid nearby, Cruz grabbed one of the newspapers he was selling and leaned against one of the windows as if waiting for someone. Julia strode to the counter he'd told her about, handed over the passport he'd given her, then began a discussion with the woman standing behind the computer screen. As Julia spoke, the attendant nodded then she began to type. She pointed to the screen a second later and then ducked beneath her station. When she stood, she held an envelope out to Julia.

Julia took so long to accept the tickets, Cruz began to think she wasn't going to, but she did reach out with an unsteady hand. Walking away from the counter, the ticket gripped tightly, she found a chair and sat down.

Seconds stretched into minutes before she opened what she held. She scanned the ticket and boarding pass, then she raised her head and looked around the terminal. This was his last chance, a small, still voice said in the back of Cruz's mind. *If you're going to do anything, you need to do it now.*

He flipped a page of the newspaper and glanced in her direction. She was fingering the ticket and staring off into the distance, a dozen different emotions crossing her face. Cruz felt ill. She thought the whole thing was a trick and she couldn't decide what to do. If she saw him, she might run. As far as Cruz knew, Guillermo and Amalia were where he'd left them but who knew for how long. If Julia fled the airport and they got out, disaster might follow.

Cruz couldn't risk approaching her.

After another long moment, Julia stood and headed for the security gate. Following her at a safe distance, Cruz waited until she boarded the plane.

Only when the jet turned into a speck in the bright blue sky did he leave.

CHAPTER SIXTEEN

THE TOCUMEN AIRPORT in Panama City was beautiful. Modern, clean and airy, the building was a testament to the power of commerce and free enterprise. Julia didn't notice, though. She exited passport control with eyes for Portia and Tomas and nothing more. Searching the faces of the people waiting for the passengers, she didn't see them and her heart started pounding in panic. From San Isidro to Medellin to Panama City, she'd fingered the note she'd found with her ticket, reading it over and over. The handwriting had looked like Portia's and what she'd written had sounded like her, but Julia didn't trust herself enough to be sure.

And she sure as hell didn't trust Jonathan Cruz.

When she hadn't been reading the note, she'd worried herself sick with thoughts of Tomas. Literally. After throwing up for the third time, she'd had to force herself to think of something other than her son. Her thoughts had immediately turned to the man who'd come into her life so unexpectedly and who'd proceeded to turn it upside down.

He'd betrayed her in every possible way.

Or had he?

While she'd been trapped in the jail, not knowing what would happen next, Julia had focused all her rage on Cruz, but now she wasn't as convinced as she had been that Cruz had used her. He'd helped her escape, but had he set up Julia for Miguel's murder? Had he been working with Guillermo and Amalia all along? Had he used her or had he saved her life? If he had framed her, then why get her out of jail?

The questions fled her mind when she heard her name. Turning to the sound with a mixture of both fear and hope, she spotted Portia. In her arms was Tomas. Joy and relief surged through her, and she ran to sweep her son into her arms, her tears beginning before she even pressed him to her.

Only after she had Tomas safely locked in her embrace did she realize who stood on either side of Portia.

Her parents and Meredith.

Her mouth dropped open in shock as Julia met their eyes. "Daddy? Mother? Meredith! Oh, my God! You're all here! I can't believe it!"

With a cry of her own, Elsa Vandamme pulled Julia against her, her hug as tight and protective as the one Julia had on her own son. When Phillip Vandamme joined them and made the circle complete, Julia was overwhelmed.

There were no words to describe the way she felt,

and that led to thoughts of Cruz. He'd never had this kind of love. Never. He'd had no one. No parents. No wife. No children.

The idea jarred her, and then it was gone, brushed aside by Meredith's embrace. Her friend held on tight and whispered in her ear. "Are you okay? I mean *really* okay?"

Julia answered through her tears. "I am now," she said. "With friends like you, how could I not be?" She sniffed. "But God, Meredith, how did you do all this—"

Julia's mother interrupted, gesturing toward Meredith. "She phoned us as soon as Portia called her and told her what had happened. We took the next flight out of Miami."

Meredith smiled back with a bland expression. "That's right," she said meeting Julia's eyes. "That's right." *And don't ask me anything else right now,* her expression said. *I'll explain everything later...*

Putting aside her queries, Julia turned in gratitude to Portia. "My God, Portia, you've done so much. Thank you for all the help, all the support. All the—"

She shook her head. "It wasn't me, sweetheart. It was Cruz. He's the one who came to me after you were arrested and told me to call your friend. He had tickets, the passports. He'd even taken Miguel's address book from his desk."

She held out an expensive leather-bound journal. Held shut with a rubber band, it was stuffed with pa-

pers and what looked like old letters. Still holding
Tomas, Julia took it then pulled out one of the enve-
lopes.

Her name was on the front and her parents' address was in the left-hand corner. The date stamped
on the top was from the year before.

Miguel had intercepted all their letters.

Julia faltered, but she'd decided long before that
if she ever got free, she wouldn't let Miguel continue
to pervert her. Not after all he'd done to her. This was
her first test of that resolve, and she surprised herself by putting the bitterness behind her. That time
of her life was over. It was done.

Meredith interceded and began to herd them toward
the exit where she already had a black SUV and a
driver waiting. Julia gave the man behind the wheel a
fast glance. He wore sunglasses and an earpiece and
met her stare with a quick look of his own. Two other
men, his twins in size and attitude, stood near the rear
of the vehicle. They were bodyguards, she realized
with a start. She looked at Meredith, confusion in her
eyes, but her friend shook her head and mouthed,
Later...

Jets thundered as Meredith and Phillip climbed
into the front seat while Julia, Portia and Elsa got into
the back. Tomas, still clinging to Julia's neck, looked
up at the sky and laughed.

"Airplane, Mama, airplane!"

The car joined traffic while they all laughed at the

little boy's innocent comment. After everything he'd been through, an airplane taking off could still manage to claim his attention.

For that, Julia was thankful. With some good luck and a lot of love, maybe that would be all he'd remember.

As if reading her thoughts, her mother squeezed her fingers. "He'll be fine," she said with authority. "Kids are tougher than we give them credit for."

"How about their mothers?" Julia asked.

"I don't know." Elsa's blue eyes, mirrors of Julia's, filled suddenly. "I think their children's ordeals are more trying on them than we realize."

"What about fathers?" Phillip looked back at the two women. "We always get short shrift," he complained. "No one thinks about us staying up late and wearing out the carpet."

Julia took his hand. "You're right," she said. "You don't get enough credit. If I'd listened to you in the first place, this nightmare would never have happened. I'll never forget that, Daddy."

Her father·squeezed her hand. "I love you," he said in a thick voice. "And you and Tomas are home. That's all that matters now."

Julia nodded, her throat tight. "You're right. But I'll make sure your grandson knows how smart you are. I'm going to need help raising him, you know. I think you might be exactly what he needs."

"And what about me?" Meredith complained,

breaking the moment. "Don't adopted aunties have rights, too?"

The mood lightened with that. The very ordinariness of the situation felt wonderful, but at the same time Julia felt torn, a thousand contradictory emotions hitting her. She was sad and happy. Thrilled and scared. Worried and relieved. On top of those feelings were her thoughts of Cruz. They wouldn't leave her, and she wondered if they ever would.

She didn't release Tomas until the men Meredith had hired were in place outside the door, then Julia relented and let the child down from her arms. He immediately ran to a pile of new toys, some of which still bore stickers from the American toy store where his grandparents had obviously purchased them before leaving the States.

Julia told herself her mother was right. Tomas probably wouldn't even remember his ordeal. He would grow up an American and hear stories about his fine Colombian father who died when Tomas was only a baby.

He'd never know they were lies.

PORTIA WENT TO BED early, but the rest of them talked until they were hoarse. After dinner, Julia pried Tomas's attention away from his new toys and brought him to her side until he fell asleep on the couch. Her hand brushing his hair, she looked up at her parents and shook her head. "I can't believe we're all back together again. I can't believe we're here."

"You have Meredith to thank for that," Julia's father said, nodding toward the woman who sat at the other end of the couch. "Without her help, this reunion wouldn't be taking place. She arranged our charter and everything."

Julia shifted her gaze to her friend, speculation in her eyes and her voice. "She *is* pretty remarkable, isn't she? And to think all this happened just because we ran into each other in Bogota. Isn't that amazing?"

"It truly is." Not reacting to Julia's tone, Elsa Vandamme rose from her chair and gestured to Tomas. "But we can talk it all out some more tomorrow. That grandson of mine needs to be put in bed."

Julia started to jump to her feet, but then she saw the expression of longing on her mother's face. "Would you like to get him ready, Mom?"

Her mother's eyes filled and her voice cracked. "Oh, sweetheart, nothing would please me more!"

Julia smiled through her own. "Then I'll concede tonight. But tomorrow he's mine."

They hugged briefly then Elsa picked up the little boy. With Phillip's arm around her, they headed for one of the bedrooms, the door closing softly behind them.

It was the first time the two old friends had been alone, and Julia took a deep breath. "I'll never be able to repay you for what you did for me, Meredith. I owe you so much—"

"It was nothing," Meredith said. "You would have done the same for me."

"I would have if I could have," Julia replied. "But I don't think I've got what it takes. I have so many questions about everything that happened..."

"That's fine," Meredith said quietly. "Ask away. Just don't expect too many answers."

"Why not?"

"I might not have them."

"And if you do..."

She met Julia's eyes. "And if I do, I still might not be able to give them to you, Julia. I know that's hard to accept, but the people I got to help me with your problem aren't exactly average citizens."

Julia barked out a laugh. "Tell me something I *don't* know. I've never met anyone in my life like Jonathan Cruz. He's..." Her voice died out. She couldn't think of a word that described the man who'd saved her son and stolen her heart.

Meredith's expression softened. "Cruz is a good guy, Julia. If you take anything away from this, take that."

Julia stood and went to the windows, her back to her friend. Afraid she'd generate some questions herself, she didn't want Meredith to see her expression. "Where *did* you find him?" she asked.

"I have contacts," Meredith said casually. "From my days with the CIA. I thought he could help."

"I thought he might be connected to your business."

Meredith laughed lightly. "Why would you think that? Does Cruz act like a financial adviser?"

Julia turned. "No. But I don't think that's what you do, either."

Meredith shrugged.

"Did you send him to kill Miguel?"

"I was concerned for you." She dodged the question. "I told him to do what he had to in order to help you escape. When I saw you at the party, I knew you had to get out of there quickly."

"He asked me to help him kill Miguel," she said, anguish in her voice. "I told him I would if he could get Tomas and me out."

Meredith answered with perfect calm. They could have been discussing what to order for dinner. "If Cruz thought that was what needed to be done, then you did the right thing by agreeing. He isn't the kind of guy who makes mistakes."

"Did he kill Miguel?"

"I can't answer that. I wasn't there."

"Well, what happened after I was arrested? How did Cruz know—"

Meredith held up her hand and stopped her. "I don't know the details, Julia. I really don't. He called me and let me know that Tomas was coming out and I jumped on the plane. Whatever went down, went down on Cruz's watch. You'll have to ask him."

"Will he have more answers for me than you?"

She smiled. "I doubt it."

"Did you set up the meeting on the street between us?"

"Yes, I did," she said. "My father told me your parents hadn't heard from you in a long time and I was concerned. I had a friend keep an eye on the flights out of San Isidro. When he saw your name on the passenger list, he called me."

Julia raised an eyebrow. "You have quite a few friends."

Meredith stood and came to her side. "Actually, I only have one or two," she said. "That's why I have to keep such a close eye on them."

"Is Cruz one of them?"

She nodded slowly. "Cruz *is* one of them. We've known each other for a long time."

"But he has secrets."

"Don't we all?"

Julia glanced sharply at her friend. "Not like he does," she said. "Not like *you* do," then she added, "superwoman…"

Meredith ignored the nickname. "He's a very brave man, Julia. And he's tough, in case you hadn't noticed."

"Oh, I noticed," Julia said. "I noticed that and a lot of other things, too. I owe him my life and Tomas's as well."

Meredith let the silence build, then she said, "You love him, don't you?"

Julia swallowed. "Is it that obvious?"

"Only to a blind man."

The two friends smiled at each other, but their expressions held no amusement. They were too weary.

Julia looked back out the window. "Will you see him?"

"Sometime. But I don't know when."

"Would you give him a message for me?"

"Of course."

"Tell him I said thank you."

Meredith put her hand on Julia's arm, her dark eyes full of sympathy. "Is that all, Julia Anne? Don't you want to—"

Julia didn't let Meredith finish. "That's it. There's nothing else to say."

MEREDITH LEFT the following day, but Portia stayed almost another week in Panama City with Julia, her parents and Tomas. When it was time for Portia to fly back to San Isidro, Julia did her best to change her friend's mind.

"I wish you'd reconsider," she said again, her hand on Portia's arm. "The place is going to be in chaos with Miguel gone. Who knows what will happen?"

"You're right," the gray-haired woman conceded. "But my home is there." She let her voice die out and then she shrugged. "I don't know. You might just open the door one day and I'll be standing on your front porch."

Julia hugged her tightly. "There's nothing I'd like more. I'm not sure I can make it without you."

"Oh, pooh!" Smiling, Portia pulled back. "You have your mother and father now. You don't need me anymore."

"I don't want you here because I *need* you," Julia replied. "I want you here because I *love* you."

"And I love you," Portia answered, "but I have to go back now."

They fell silent. Portia had been her only friend for the past few years and Julia was going to miss her. No one other than Portia would ever fully understand what Julia had experienced.

They broke apart and Portia pulled a handkerchief from her pocket and dabbed her eyes. When she faced Julia again, her composure had returned.

"Is there anything you want me to do when I get there? Anyone you want me to contact?"

Julia knew what she was implying, and pain sliced through her. "Cruz won't be in San Isidro, Portia, and even if he was, I wouldn't know what to say to him."

"He cares for you. You do know that, don't you?"

"You said that before. But I'm not convinced." Voicing the same thoughts she'd already shared with Meredith, Julia stared off into the distance and spoke with hesitation. "It's hard to imagine, standing here so far away, everything that took place, but the truth is, I agreed to help kill someone." Her gaze returned to her friend's. "And not just anyone, but the father of my son. Cruz made that happen. Whether he loves me or not almost seems irrelevant. How could *I* love him?"

"Every relationship has spots of trouble."

When Julia met Portia's amused gaze, she realized the older woman was teasing her. Julia smiled wryly. "Maybe so, but you gotta admit—"

"I admit nothing," Portia said stubbornly, "but the truth, and the truth is, he loves you."

"I don't think a man like that *can* love," Julia argued, "but it doesn't matter. He's gone. His job was over when Miguel was killed and I'm sure he's disappeared by now."

"His job was over when you flew away."

"I was a means to an end for him."

"Maybe so. But what was that end? You need to add that question to your list." She met Julia's troubled eyes. "I don't believe the answer lies solely in Miguel's death. Cruz was searching for more than that."

Remembering her earlier thoughts that Cruz might have had hidden motives, Julia tilted her head. "What do you think he was searching for?"

"I don't know. But he found you and that's what counts." She brushed Julia's cheek with a kiss. "It's just like you said, sweetie. Love always trumps need and it always will."

THE CLEANING CREW had come and gone. They'd erased all evidence of Cruz's presence in Miguel Ramirez's life, but Cruz had wanted to see the com-

pound one last time before he left San Isidro. Slipping
past the sleeping guards the government had stationed
outside the wall, he made his way to the courtyard outside the *casita* that had been Julia's bedroom, the
phone call he'd received from Meredith that afternoon
still fresh on his mind. She'd just left Panama City and
was about to fly out to check on a job in Santiago.

"They're all fine," she'd said. "I played with
Tomas, reassured the Vandammes and talked with
Julia. She's still pretty shaken up but she'll be okay."

"That's good," he'd said, his voice tight with the
questions he was holding back. How did Julia look?
What did she say? Was she feeling all right?

"She sent you a message."

He managed to sound casual. "Oh, really?"

"She sent you her...thanks."

A millisecond before Meredith said "thanks" he'd
thought she was going to say "love" and his heart did
a flip inside his chest. "That's good."

"She had a lot of questions."

"But you didn't answer them."

"Of course not. She can't ever know the whole
story."

"Well, you're more likely than I am to have future
contact with her. I won't be seeing her again, so you
can tell her I said she's welcome. It's all over now—"

"Don't."

"Don't what?"

"Don't act like nothing happened between you two. I know better."

He sat on the edge of a fountain that had been turned off and looked out the gate that Julia had opened for him. The iron bars framed the mountains beyond and the red-tiled roofs of San Isidro. Someone unfamiliar with the town would have been enchanted. Just as Julia had probably been at first. He rested his elbows on his knees, his eyes falling to the gravel where something light caught his attention. He bent down and picked up what turned out to be a crushed gardenia, lifting it to his nose.

"You fell for her."

Meredith's voice echoed inside his head. "You fell for her. Don't tell me otherwise."

"What if I did?" he had said defensively.

"You need to take care of it."

"Take care of it?"

She'd spoken with open irritation. "Don't act dense, Cruz. You know what I mean." Just in case he didn't, she explained anyway. "You need to find her and make it right."

"What makes you think I left it wrong?"

"I know you." Then she added softly, "And I know her. The two of you are the most stubborn people on the planet. That's a good thing if you're on the job, but it's a bad thing if you're in love."

"In love? C'mon, Meredith—"

"Don't," she said again.

Cruz had let the silence build because he didn't know what to say. "Go to Pascagoula," she'd ordered before she'd hung up. "They live in a big white house close to the beach, between the shipyard and the base. You can't miss it."

Cruz dropped the flower into the motionless water. The ripples were still moving as he slipped back over the wall.

HER FATHER KEPT the bodyguards for another month. Julia had tried to get him to let them go but he refused. "Don't worry about it," he'd said. "I feel more comfortable with them around."

"But it's getting expensive."

"Trouble would cost more."

That had sounded like something Cruz would have said, but Julia hadn't pressed her dad. Another month passed and he finally let them go.

Upon their departure, however, he hired a nanny. Ms. Barclay's shoulders were as wide as those on the bodyguards and her jacket never quite fit over the bulge under her arm. She was great with Tomas, though, and he loved her so Julia had said nothing more.

In fact, she said little about anything, choosing instead to let her father make the decisions and let her mother care for them. The results had been immediately obvious. Tomas had blossomed under his grandparents' love and Ms. Barclay's watch. He'd even begun to talk more in English.

A few e-mails had made their way to Julia from Portia. She'd gotten home just fine, she'd said, and San Isidro was still San Isidro. Guillermo and Amalia had been transferred to Bogota for their trial but Portia expected they would pay off the judge and return within a few years. In the meantime, a minor lieutenant who'd been one of Miguel's favorites had taken over the business. When Guillermo and Amalia did return, more blood would be shed until they took over again.

Portia never mentioned Cruz.

Julia tried not to notice that fact. Expecting his memory to become dimmer and dimmer until it disappeared completely she'd been shocked to discover that although it was hard to remember Miguel, she could recall every detail of her time with Cruz.

Did she love him? Were the memories she had of their closeness real or the stuff of fantasy?

Night after night Julia told herself that the truth didn't really matter and she'd repeat the few facts she did know like a mantra until she fell asleep. She and Tomas were safe. Cruz was gone and she had no way to find him. Eventually she would forget him.

Eventually…

Resolutely reaching for the computer's mouse, Julia returned to the note she'd been composing to Meredith. Her mother had a small office where she puttered, as she'd put it, but the setup was high-tech all the way, every peripheral known to man scattered across the built-in desk. Elsa could print her recipes with a color laser jet and scan them with the highest resolution. Julia had been surprised by the hardware, but decided to simply take advantage of it.

She had just hit Send when a gust of wind sprang up, setting the chimes on the balcony in motion, their soft melody a counterpoint to the ocean's waves. Lifting her head to glance toward the gaping French doors at the end of the room, she heard Ms. Barclay call Tomas's name.

The woman's voice, usually sweet and light despite the way she looked, was full of unmistakable authority. Beneath it, Julia heard fear.

Julia jumped up and ran for the double doors. Just as she reached the threshold, Ms. Barclay yelled again, this time, shockingly, in Spanish.

"Tomas! Tomas! Come back here! Right now."

Charging onto the balcony as if she could sprout wings and fly, Julia scanned her parents' generous yard. She spotted the nanny midway down the lawn. Tomas stood behind her legs, her left hand holding him still. Her right one was wrapped around a pistol and she had it pointed at a man who was frozen in front of her, his hands in the air.

Julia gasped, her heart stopping in mid-beat as fear flooded her mind and body. For one terrifying moment, she thought Miguel had come back to life, then she got herself under control and looked closer.

The man wasn't Miguel.

He was dressed in black as Miguel often did, but his body was much leaner, his jawline more defined. In the breeze from the shore, a strand of hair had fallen over his forehead but as Julia stared, the wind shifted and his face was revealed.

She whispered his name and he looked up as if he'd heard her.

"Cruz…" she breathed. "Oh, my God, it's Cruz…"

SHE WORE a white sun dress and as she crossed the lawn toward him, Cruz thought she looked as if she were floating instead of walking. The urge to sweep her into his arms hit him with such unexpected power that he felt lost, his reason for coming to see Julia nothing more than a memory.

With more resolution than he thought he had in him, Cruz pulled back and reminded himself why he was there: Meredith had been right. He needed to end things with Julia in a better way. They'd left too many questions hanging between them. The time for answers had come. When it was over, he would leave.

Regardless of his intention, though, the picture of Julia coming to him as if on a cloud of luminescence was a treasure he would never surrender. Some things, a man should never have to sacrifice.

Julia reached his side. Her eyes were bluer than he remembered, or maybe, he thought, her freedom made them look that way.

"Hello, Cruz." Her Southern drawl seemed more pronounced, too.

"Hello, Julia." He nodded toward Tomas and the gun-toting nanny, who, despite Julia's dismissal, was still eyeing him suspiciously as she guided her charge down to the beach. "That's some nursemaid you've got."

"My dad hired her."

"Smart man. Tomas is growing. I heard him talking, too. In English."

When she smiled, her whole face lit up, something he hadn't seen in Colombia.

"He's doing so well," she said. "I thank God every day for the way he's recovered. I don't think he'll even remember what happened."

"Then you should tell him." Cruz saw her frown. "Everyone needs to know where they came from, Julia. That's how you measure how far you've traveled."

She folded her arms. "Where you are today is all that's important. The past doesn't matter."

He wondered if she believed what she'd just said. "Then I'm wasting my time. I came here to clear up a few things between us, but if the past means nothing, I might as well turn around and go now."

For a brief moment, he thought she was going to agree with him then her face seemed to soften. "I can't let you leave just like that," she said. "This is the South, you know. We have our standards as far as hospitality goes. If I don't invite you in, my mother will think I didn't learn any manners at all."

"We can't have her believing that," he said.

Their eyes met and both of them acknowledged her lie for what it was. A moment later, she led him toward the white clapboard house. A huge porch ran the length of it and by the time they reached it, Phillip Vandamme was waiting. His wife, Julia's mother, Elsa, stood beside him. And they both looked suspicious.

Julia made the introductions, but Vandamme's attitude didn't change. He shook Cruz's hand, though, and then Elsa steered them all to a group of padded chairs on the porch. They could never act as if they knew anything about him. Revealing their part in the whole affair would put the lives of hundreds of operatives in danger. All they "knew" was what Julia had told them. She went inside, murmuring something about getting cold drinks.

"We appreciate what you did for our daughter and grandson." Phillip looked over his shoulder to make sure Julia was out of earshot. "You'll never know the depth of our gratitude."

His own emotions in turmoil, Cruz replied, "I think I have an idea."

"You risked your life for her—and for us," Julia's mother said flatly. "We know what that means and we won't ever forget it."

Surprised by her reference to his job, Cruz turned

to her. In her face he could see Julia's future. Elsa Vandamme was a beautiful woman but even more important, at least to Cruz, was the strength of character that shone in her eyes. "But she can't ever learn—"

Cruz interrupted her with a shake of his head. "She won't, not from me."

Phillip changed the subject, clearly uneasy with his wife's bluntness. "Will you be staying in the States for a while, Mr. Cruz, or do you have your next job lined up already?"

Was her father worried that Cruz had come to take Julia away as easily as he'd restored her to them?

He tried to sound reassuring. "Actually, I don't know what I'm going to do—"

The screen door squeaked before he could finish and Julia stepped out carrying a tray of glasses and a pitcher of iced tea. Cruz jumped up and took the tray from her hands, placing it on the low table. She sat down beside him.

"I don't know what I'm going to do next," he resumed. "I've left the organization I was with and I'm not quite sure what I'll be doing."

Julia froze at his words. "You quit working?"

"When you do what I did, quitting isn't an option," he said quietly. "Let's just say, I'm moving on."

"Why?"

From the corner of his eye, Cruz saw Phillip

Vandamme tilt his head. The almost imperceptible movement sent Elsa Vandamme to her feet.

"I'm sorry to be so rude," she said smoothly to Cruz, "but we've got rosebushes in the front of the house that absolutely have to be trimmed today. The only reason I let Phillip take the day off was so he'd do them for me. If I don't get him out there soon, he's going to find an excuse to escape the task." She sent a look to her husband and he got up with a patently fake expression of guilt. She held her hand out to Cruz. When he took her fingers in his, she covered them with her other hand. "We'd love to have you stay for lunch so we can visit more, though. Could you manage it?"

"I'd like to," he said, "but I have to take a rain check."

Clearly sensing that something was up, her eyes flicked to Julia then went back to Cruz. "That's too bad," she said. "Perhaps we'll have another opportunity?"

He smiled and shrugged, then Julia's parents went back inside, the screen door slamming behind them.

"Why did you quit?" Julia repeated her question.

"It was time," he said.

She waited for more, but he gave her nothing else.

"I don't understand," she said. "I don't understand why you quit or why you're here or what we're doing right now. I don't understand any of it and I've been in a fog ever since I left San Isidro." Her voice cracked as her frustration, pent up for too long, spilled over. "I don't understand and I'm so confused."

Cruz pulled her into his arms, her moment of resistance giving way as quickly as his promise to himself to keep his distance. They didn't kiss, though. This wasn't the time for that.

"I'm not sure I understand, either," he confessed. "But there were mistakes made in Colombia, and I always said I'd quit when that started to happen. Getting careless is a fast way to die, and I'm not interested in doing that just yet."

Julia raised her head, and he steeled himself against the questions he knew were coming.

"I have to ask," she said.

"I know," he answered. "That's why I came."

"Did you kill Miguel?"

"No."

"Who did?"

"Jorge Guillermo."

"Why?"

"Amalia Riveria told him to. They were planning to take over Miguel's empire." He touched Julia's cheek, then continued. "It was Guillermo who came into your room that night. They were going to kidnap you to create a diversion."

As if she needed more space to absorb the truth, Julia eased out of his embrace, but she didn't go far. It was a reflection of how they both felt, he realized.

The push-pull of their uneasy relationship a factor too large to be ignored.

"How do I know you're telling the truth?" she asked.

He took her hands in his. "The day we went to get Tomas, when we were in the jungle, do you remember what happened when you surprised me?"

Her cheeks paled, and she swallowed. "You almost broke my neck."

"That's right. I put my hand on the side of your head and my arm across your throat."

Her eyes met his but he didn't blink.

"That's what I do, Julia," he said. "I kill people by breaking their necks. I don't use a weapon and I never have. Guns aren't fail-safe. They make noise and other people can grab them and use them against you." He paused. "I would have broken Miguel's neck. He was shot."

His stark words seemed to take away any remaining doubts she had. Cruz hated himself for explaining things to her in such an unforgiving manner, but it was the only way she'd know for sure. He knew this because he'd devoted countless days worrying over how to convince her and he'd come up with nothing but this.

The truth.

She blinked. "You didn't set me up?"

"No," he said again. "I came to the compound that night to get you out of there. I'd decided that I should never have asked you for your help. It wasn't fair and

I shouldn't have burdened you that way. I was going to get you out of there and return to kill Miguel. When I checked your door and saw that it was locked, though, something didn't seem right. I went on to the main part of the villa to figure out what was going on. That's when I realized Guillermo had already sent everyone home, but I didn't know why. When I went to Miguel's *casita,* I understood."

"Miguel was already dead?"

"Yes." Cruz nodded. "I was trying to decide what to do next when someone came up behind me and knocked me out."

He'd already decided against telling her about seeing Amalia's shoes and having doubts. Thinking back on it now, he wondered how he could have ever been suspicious of Julia. He traced the line of her shoulder with his finger. "It was Guillermo. He dragged me to the hole at the back of the compound and dumped me in. All Amalia had to do after that was unlock your door and call the *policia.*"

"How did you get out?"

He explained and when he finished, all she could do was shake her head. "So much violence," she whispered. "So much death."

He cupped his hands around her face. "But look what came out of it," he said. "You're free, Tomas is free, Guillermo and Amalia are in jail, for a while, anyway. It had to be done, Julia."

He wished he could tell her about the DEA men

whose lives had been saved as well, but that had to remain as much a secret as her parents' involvement.

She seemed to read his mind. "I understand what you're saying, Cruz, but I still have questions and one of them is why me? Miguel could have picked any woman in the world to do this to. Why did he choose me?"

Cruz couldn't lie. Not now. But he couldn't tell her the truth, either. Julia could never learn of her parents' secret life. He put his hands on either side of her face and held her still.

"Why *not* you?" he asked. "You're beautiful, you're smart, any man in his right mind would want you, Julia."

She put her hands on his. "That's not good enough and you know it. I think Miguel picked me for a reason. I meant something to him. He pursued me." Her eyes went over his shoulder then back to Cruz's face. "He chased me down, then he caught me and tortured me, just like a cat does a mouse. If I'd been there much longer, he would have killed me and finished it."

"He was crazy, Julia. Leave it at that or you'll drive yourself to the same conclusion."

She considered his advice, her face showing her confusion. Even though she'd demanded answers, part of her didn't really want to know. Miguel had been capable of a cruelty that few people understood and Julia knew this better than anyone. The burden of his reasoning would be a heavy load for her to carry the rest of her life. She closed her eyes.

"You have secrets," she said finally.

"And I always will."

They stared at each other.

"We come from very different worlds," he said after a moment.

"And that won't ever change," she replied.

Her eyes went to the water's edge and Cruz followed her gaze. The woman who'd pointed a gun at him had taken Tomas to the shore to build a sand castle.

"He's first in my life." Julia nodded toward the little boy.

"As he should be," Cruz said.

He waited a few more moments, then Cruz stood and pulled Julia to her feet. He'd faced death with less trepidation, but if he was going to take the risk, the time had come. He held her hands tightly and lost himself in her blue eyes.

"There's one secret I can't keep from you," he said.

She waited.

"I told you how I grew up," he started. "You know all about me. I've never had a family and I don't think I even know what it means to be a part of one. I came here today to tell you that and to try to make you see why it would be best if we went our separate ways."

She stared at him calmly.

"I'm not a good man and I've done some terrible

things. I've seen a side of life that no one should even know exists. Miguel Ramirez and I were more alike than we were different—"

"That's not true."

"It *is* true, but there's one important difference, I'm smarter than he was, and I've learned something too important to pretend as if I don't know. And that's where the secret comes in."

He paused, then took the plunge. "I love you," he said. "I think I did from the moment I saw you. I couldn't let myself think about what that meant at the time but now it's all I can think about."

She started to say something but he placed a finger across her lips.

"I don't know what kind of future we could have, but I'd like it to be one that we share. I've been approached by the government to teach some classes at Langley. I'd like the three of us to go there together—you, me and Tomas."

Gripping his hands with an almost painful strength, Julia shook her head, her eyes gleaming. Cruz started to get worried, then he read her expression and he felt lighter than he ever had before.

"Was that a proposal?" she asked.

Cruz grinned uncertainly. "I think it might have been." Tilting his head, he acted as if he were considering something. "Yeah, yeah, I think it was."

"Then I think my answer is yes," she said. "I'm willing to try if you are."

Over the roar of the waves, Tomas's laughter reached them. Cruz smiled at the sound then he lowered his head and kissed Julia, their future no secret at all.

* * * * *

Turn the page for an excerpt from
NOT WITHOUT THE TRUTH,
the next book in THE OPERATIVES *series*
by Kay David.

NOT WITHOUT THE TRUTH
(Harlequin Superromance #1321)
is available in January 2006.

PROLOGUE

Christmas Eve, 1989
American Consulate
Lima, Peru

LAUREN WAS SUPPOSED to be asleep by 9:00 p.m., but Lauren didn't always follow the rules. In fact, she *seldom* followed the rules, especially dumb ones that didn't make any sense to begin with. It was Christmas Eve. Who went to bed at nine on Christmas Eve?

Her mother had said ten-year-old girls did. At least those who wanted to find presents under the tree in the morning.

Margaret Stanley had tried to appear stern and serious as she'd said that, but Lauren had heard the softness behind those words. They both knew that despite how Lauren behaved, her Christmas was going to be a good one. Six months ago, her mom had been appointed the new consul for Peru, and she felt guilty for making Lauren and her dad have to come halfway across the world. Lauren had seen the stack of presents her mom had already wrapped.

Lauren played along, though. After her mom kissed her good-night and turned down the lamp, she closed her eyes and waited ten minutes, then she climbed out of bed. Sneaking into the hallway, she peered both ways before running to the iron railing that lined the upper gallery. She was immediately rewarded for her misbehavior.

A crowd filled the huge reception area below, but as if he'd planned it, Daniel Cunningham, her mother's attaché, stood directly beneath the spot where Lauren knelt. His tuxedo was pressed, his shoes shone, and he'd spiked his blond hair for the party. The style made him look even taller than he was and, gripping the black balusters, Lauren pressed her face between the bars and sighed.

Okay, so he was old—at least twenty, maybe even twenty-five—*and* he worked for her mom, but he was *sooo* cool! Lauren had had a major crush on Daniel since the minute they'd arrived.

Normally her mom would have had a cow over Lauren's thing for Daniel, but she'd overheard her parents talking, and her mom had admitted she was giving Lauren a break because Daniel had managed to distract her. Lauren had bawled for days when she'd found out she was going to have to leave all her friends. Knowing there was no chance, she'd even begged to stay with her grandparents instead of moving. "We're a family," her mother had said. "And that means we stick together." Lauren had been really, really bummed. Until she'd spotted Daniel.

Daniel liked her, too. He treated her like she had some sense, not like she was just some kid who didn't have a choice about where she lived. He'd even taken the time to explain to her why it was important that she and her dad be there. Her mother was the consul, Daniel had said solemnly, but the people of Peru saw the entire family as representatives of the United States. Daniel made her think she counted, something her mother never had the time to do.

Her mother came into view. She'd let Lauren pick out her dress for tonight, but neither had been surprised by the one she'd selected. The red beaded gown was Lauren's favorite, and it fit her mom perfectly, the crystals shimmering as she walked among her guests. She looked like a movie star, or maybe even a model. They didn't always get along, but her mom was really pretty neat and she was definitely awesome looking.

In contrast, her father bobbed behind her mother like the little boat Lauren had played with in the bathtub when she was a kid. He had on a tux like the other men, but the similarities stopped there. He wasn't elegant or even handsome and he sure didn't seem to be having a good time. Maybe it was his glasses that made him look that way. More likely, it was his frown. Her father was a child psychiatrist and back home, he'd taught other doctors at a fancy medical center how to treat crazy kids. He hadn't ever been a fun kind of dad, but since they'd come to South America, he'd stopped smiling completely. She'd even heard him yell at her mom once, something he'd never done in Dallas. Tonight he looked even more uptight than usual.

He pretended he didn't see Lauren as she peeked out from behind the railing. He was mad at her, she knew, because she'd been such a toot about moving.

Her eyes searched the mob again. Daniel had moved closer to the dining room, she saw, and another man, dressed in black, was standing beside him. She looked at Daniel but her gaze kept returning to the other man. He was shorter than Daniel and Latin, his wide shoulders filling out his jacket with muscles that Daniel could only dream of ever having. His black hair was long and slicked back and as she watched, he reached up and smoothed it, a gleam of gold on his wrist catching her attention. He looked…kinda rough, she decided, unsophisticated in comparison to the blond attaché. Like those guys on TV who always played the drug lords.

Without thinking, Lauren edged closer to the balusters so she could see better and when she did so, Daniel glanced up, the white of her nightgown obviously drawing his notice. He smiled at her and lifted his glass as if in a salute. She wagged her fingers back at him, her heart doing a funny skipping thing inside her chest.

The man at Daniel's side turned and raised his eyes, too. Lauren glanced in his direction then something weird seemed to happen.

He was younger than she'd first thought, but his eyes didn't match the rest of him. They looked more like the old man's on the corner. The one who sold newspapers. He was about a hundred years old and he never smiled, not even when Lauren's dad gave him twice as big a tip as he should. Lauren's delight in being acknowledged by Daniel changed to confusion. The man's scrutiny scared her.

Suddenly it seemed like a good time for Lauren to go.

She jumped to her feet, her gown billowing around her legs, laughter and music from downstairs chasing her back to the private area of the embassy. Her pulse racing as fast as her feet, she found herself in her mother's closet a few moments later, the familiar scent of perfume as reassuring as Lauren needed it to be. She sat down on the floor behind the louvered doors and waited for the jittery feeling to leave.

She kept telling herself she wasn't afraid until she fell into a fitful sleep, her dreams full of men with gold eyes. When she woke up to loud voices, it took her a moment to remember where she was.

"Dammit, Margaret...you don't understand.... Big mistake if you think... Lots of money to be made..."

Lauren started to call out, but the angry words held her back. Peeking through the doors, all she could see were a pair of men's shoes and the hem of her mother's red gown. The man kinda sounded like Daniel but not really. Daniel never used bad words like "dammit" and his voice was much deeper than this man's.

"...not in the foreign service for money. I love my country..."

Lauren teased her mom sometimes and called her "General Mother." No matter what, she stayed the same: strong, brave, no-nonsense. She was acting that way now. Taking a step toward the closet door, her mother still spoke. "You aren't going to get away with this. I found out and others will, too."

"They won't if you aren't talking."

The man had come nearer, too, but Lauren still couldn't tell if it was Daniel or not. He sounded really scary, which made her think about the stranger she'd seen beside Daniel. The man with the brace-let. Lauren heard him pull something from his pocket.

Her mother's gasp turned Lauren's stomach inside out, and she gripped a handful of carpet, her mouth going dust dry.

Her mother spoke slowly and calmly, just like she did when she was trying to explain something to Lauren. "Don't be stupid. That's not going to help things."

"I can see how you'd feel that way," the man said. "But I disagree."

A muffled pop followed.

Lauren was scrambling backward before the sound faded. She bumped into the farthest wall, then squeezed her eyes shut. Wedging herself as deep as she could into the darkness, she tried not to think about what that noise meant. Part of her understood, but a desperate sense of survival kept her silent. Over the crazy ringing in her ears, she thought she heard the bedroom door open and close but she couldn't tell for sure, especially when she heard the sound again a few minutes later. Rocking back and forth, she moaned softly.

Five minutes passed. Maybe five hours.

Her mother always preached that procrastination only made things worse, but something told Lauren "worse" was on the other side of the closet door this time. She waited for as long as she dared, then she forced herself to uncurl her legs. One way or the other, she had to find out what had happened. She crawled on all fours like the baby she wished she still was until she reached the front of the closet. Taking a deep breath, she pushed the doors open.

Her mother lay on the floor, a red pool the color of her dress staining the carpet by her head.

A man bent over her, two fingers pressed to her throat. He wore black from head to toe, including a mask that completely covered his head.

A gun was on the floor beside her mother's outstretched arm.

Through the eye holes of the mask, the man's startled gaze met Lauren's. He jerked his hand away from her mother's neck and a gold glint on his wrist caught Lauren's attention.

For one long second, Lauren was frozen. She couldn't move, she couldn't talk, she couldn't even breathe. The man went still, too.

Lauren didn't understand what happened next, but she knew she'd never forget it. She could hear his heartbeat, she realized with shock, and the quick intake of breath that *he* took filled *her* lungs. He sensed the connection, as well. His dark eyes came alive, their earlier flatness replaced with surprise.

Suddenly he pivoted and dashed to the nearest window. Lauren closed her eyes and began to scream.

HARLEQUIN *Super*ROMANCE®

**A powerful new story from a
RITA® Award-nominated author!**

A Year and a Day
by **Inglath Cooper**

**Harlequin Superromance #1310
On sale November 2005**

Audrey Colby's life is the envy of most. She's
married to a handsome, successful man, she
has a sweet little boy and they live in a lovely
home in an affluent neighborhood. But
everything is not always as it seems. Only
Nicholas Wakefiled has seen the danger
Audrey's in. Instead of helping, though,
he complicates things even more....

Available wherever Harlequin books are sold.

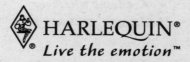

HARLEQUIN®
Live the emotion™

An Unlikely Match
by Cynthia Thomason

Harlequin Superromance #1312
On sale November 2005

She's the mayor of Heron Point. He's an
uptight security expert. When Jack Hogan
tells Claire Betancourt that her little town
of artisans and free spirits has a security
problem, sparks fly! Then her daughter goes
missing, and Claire knows that Jack is the
man to bring her safely home.

Available wherever
Harlequin books are sold.

HARLEQUIN®

AMERICAN *Romance*®

Presenting...

CHRISTMAS, TEXAS STYLE

A holiday gift for readers of
Harlequin American Romance

Novellas from three of
your favorite authors

Four Texas Babies
TINA LEONARD

A Texan Under the Mistletoe
LEAH VALE

Merry Texmas
LINDA WARREN

*Available November 2005 wherever
Harlequin books are sold.*

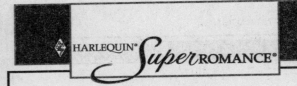

HARLEQUIN *Super*ROMANCE®

Critically acclaimed author

Tara Taylor Quinn

brings you

The Promise
of Christmas

**Harlequin Superromance #1309
On sale November 2005**

In this deeply emotional story, a woman
unexpectedly becomes the guardian of her
brother's child. Shortly before Christmas,
Leslie Sanderson finds herself coping with
grief, with lingering and fearful memories and
with unforseen motherhood. She also
rediscovers a man from her past who could
help her move toward the promise
of a new future....

Available wherever Harlequin books are sold.

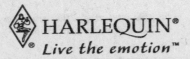

HARLEQUIN®
Live the emotion™